DIVE
DEEP
and
DEADLY

DIVE DEEP and DEADLY

by
Glynn Marsh Alam

MEMENTO MORI MYSTERY

Memento Mori Mysteries
Published by
Avocet Press Inc
19 Paul Court
Pearl River, NY 10965
http://www.avocetpress.com
mysteries@avocetpress.com

AVOCET PRESS

Library of Congress Cataloging-in-Publication Data

Alam, Glynn Marsh, 1943-
  Dive deep and deadly : a Luanne Fogarty mystery / by Glynn Marsh
Alam.-- 1st ed.
    p. cm.
  ISBN 0-9661072-9-2
  1. Women detectives--Florida--Tallahassee Region--Fiction. 2. Tallahassee Region (Fla.)-
-Fiction. 3. Linguistics teachers--Fiction. 4. Scuba diving--Fiction. I. Title.
  PS3551.L213 D58 2000
  813'.54--dc21
                              99-050928

Cover Photographs:
  Cave Diving - copyright © 1999 Ken McDonald and Pat Kennedy
  Swamp - copyright © 1999 Glynn Marsh Alam
  Author - copyright © 1999 Melodie Earickson

Printed in the USA
First Edition

To U.B. and Clara Marsh

They call us the spring people. Those of us who live down from Tallahassee, by the Palmetto River, too far down to notice the tourists on the glass bottom boats at the main spring. Swamp folk. Our neighbors are reptilian sometimes, buggy most of the time. We live in the world of screens that hold out mosquitoes and gnats in the oppressing mugginess that sits atop us in the evenings. Even in winter time when bugs fold up, the layer of damp air hovers above the swamp floor, above the still parts of the springs, especially where the sinkhole waters rest on tenuous ground—uneasy sand, water, mist. Every few years, the whole thing drops out like the devil has pulled the plug. Anything on top of the water goes with it, right down to nowhere, maybe to the ocean. No one has ever tracked it far enough to know. All the springs offshoot from the Palmetto, a long primeval forest river that has gouged out limestone caverns for millions of years along its trek to the Gulf of Mexico. Glacier cold water filters into the springs, places for catfish the size of dogs, and alligators that travel to the depths to drown baby deer before surfacing to gulp them down in jaws that cannot chew. These same alligators raise their young on the dead grass that floats atop the still waters of little inlets around giant cypress trees. But the springs are not still. Cold water jets up from depths no one has ever seen, cold, and plentiful enough to service a hotel built in the thirties for those rich enough to escape the Great Depression.

I live in my family home, the gray wood house closest to Fogarty Spring. I have reclaimed a structure left to rot and throw its ghosts to the jungle, returned to the grunting calls of mama gators searching for lost babies, to sucker-footed rain frogs that infest the bushes outside my window and occasionally travel inside with me. A poisonous water moccasin crawls underneath my steep front steps to cool itself away from the steaming heat of day.

I have, once again, become one of the spring people. If I am lucky, and treat it kindly, the swamp will let me stay.

CHAPTER ONE

"Ms. Fogarty, the fellows from the sheriff's department want you to come down to the main spring if you can." Dorian Pasquin stood on my front steps, fanning himself with the tattered straw hat, an appendage to an invisible umbilical at his crown. "They say it's urgent." This man, his skin broken to dried-up mud patch consistency and tanned from river work in his youth, broke into a white-toothed grin. Those teeth, all his own, appeared like shiny pearls inside a mud oyster. His full shock of white hair lay plastered in humid strands about his ears, except for the very top of his head, where it stood up like a cockatoo's crest. In a rigid stance, he may have reached my shoulders. During his eighty-plus years, survived in a critter-filled swamp, he had taken on the demeanor of its inhabitants. In spite of his age, he stooped only at the neck. Pasquin moved with the swamp, slow and easy and deliberate, aware of the broken twig behind him, the silvery spider web in front. He was also the nearest neighbor in Fogarty Spring with a phone. I hadn't been here long enough to get the phone company to run a line to my house.

"What's happened? Another drowning, or another Yankee gone snorkeling and got himself on a gator's dinner table?"

"Don't know, ma'am. I just answered the phone, and they

says to come runnin'. Maybe you just better do it." Pasquin's Cajun twang had to be one of the last in this area, and how he kept it with so few Cajuns around was a linguistic wonder. But no locals wondered. He was just Pasquin—a *Kay-June* man. He has always called me ma'am, like an old man playing with his grandchild.

"Can I go to your place and call them back? Likely they want me to bring diving equipment, and I don't relish driving all the way back over that muddy road."

"Sho' can, ma'am, just walk along with me. Saw two copper-heads on the way over. You got something 'sides them sandals?"

I looked down at my Birkenstocks that got me across the wooden floors for hours of scrubbing, repairing, and painting old boards. Sweat poured off my neck. My hair felt like a hot cloth on top of my head. Cropped short, the brown and gray tendrils stuck to my ears. I could smell my underarms without lifting them. If the sheriff wanted to see me, I hoped it would involve a swim. I could use the bath.

In ankle-high boots, my feet sticky inside the plastic mate-rial, I tugged on the warped screen door. Pasquin had sat down on one of the steps and peered between his legs.

"Ma'am, you got a long, dusty-black moccasin under here." He stressed the "sin" on moccasin. "Best you watch that thing. He bite you, you 'ain't got a phone—nasty business, ma'am." He stood up, fanned and walked in rhythm, his gaze first on the ground, then up the trees. I followed him through the forest.

The hotel clerk drawled his Southern as fast as he could. "Well, Ms. Fogarty, I think some teenage boys went diving where they ought not to and found something that scared them half out of puberty. They came running up here to the hotel and said

12

there was a body in the first cave. Cops know who the expert diver is in these springs. Said to get you down here fast. Didn't say nothing about diving gear, but I'd say you better bring it along."

"Don't they have their own divers?" I stood in a room that closed in on me. Pasquin's living room retained every piece of overstuffed furniture he had ever bought in his whole life. A frayed, dark red and green Persian rug lay over the entire floor. Heavy, green velvet curtains covered closed windows. From a back room somewhere, a powerful air conditioner blew cold air through the hall. By the time it reached the living room, it made a cold streak that bypassed the phone table altogether. My sweaty hand slid down the black, plastic receiver.

"All right. Tell them I'm on my way, but I'm going to have to load the gear, then jump some friggin' mud puddles before I get there."

The clerk grunted his understanding.

"Guess you ain't never going to get away from diving in them holes, Luanne. Don't matter if you get to be old as me, you still going in them holes." Pasquin chuckled and lifted a tea glass in my direction.

I shook my head, eager to get to the main spring and see what could be important enough to drag this forty-five-year old out of her back-breaking construction project

My '84 Honda station wagon, already loaded with pieces of lumber, some old bricks I'd picked up at a demolition site, and God knows how many packages of cafe curtains that were on sale at K Mart, could have passed for a homeless abode. When I tried to throw in scuba gear—tank, mask, hoses, flippers—it wouldn't fit. It took me twenty minutes of dumping things out,

13

carrying them to the screen porch so they wouldn't get wet if the habitual afternoon shower appeared, then hoisting the diving equipment into the wagon. Manufacturing more sweat, I had to sit down and drink an iced tea before taking off on a rutted road that had seen better days. In spots, I guided the Honda around deep puddles, placing one set of wheels precariously on a narrow shoulder. The puddle on one side, a deep ditch on the other—I have seen cars run into these ditches and nearly drown the occupants. Sometimes you can't see the water for all the reeds and grass. After a mile of this, I turned onto a dark asphalt road and hit the gas. The only witness to my speeding, a black snake trying to cross the road, hurried up when he felt the vibration of the car. I hate snakes, but I don't like killing them. Nothing humanitarian about that. It's just the wiggling under pressure that revolts me, like the thing just won't die.

When I reached the entrance to Palmetto Springs, the park ranger at the ticket booth waved me through. My back trickled with sweat and my shorts looked as though I'd peed in them; the Honda's air conditioning conked out years ago. A dip into cold water—if that's what the sheriff wanted me to do—would feel good. I panicked a little when I realized he might want me to translate for some tourist in trouble. I'd taken some French and even lived in Paris for a while. Everyone in Tallahassee thought I could speak all the dialects, including Haitian and Quebecois. My degree is in linguistics—the science of language, not the fluency of languages—but most people don't know this.

I wound through the well-manicured road that leads to the hotel bathhouse and restaurant. Gray moss hung from the trees, but not all the way to the ground, as though the gardeners wanted something of the South to be there, but not enough of it to stain the buildings, roads, and cars. I wondered just how you trimmed

14

moss to hang that way.

Pulling to a stop nearest the bathhouse, I had to walk another hundred yards to the glass bottom boat docks where a group of cops stood around, pretending to talk crime scene to each other, but most likely setting up a poker party. Whatever; it looked serious.

"We got a problem down there." The even-toned statement came from Deputy Loman, a large-bellied man whose eyes looked as if they would snap shut any minute. He pointed a thumbs down. When his superior joined us, he turned his head slightly and gazed over the spring water, his heavy lids still half-way over his eyes. If he had been a snake, his tongue would have darted in and out.

"Luanne." The monotone came from a face that looked as though it had rarely seen a dead person, though I knew otherwise. Detective Tony Amado and emotion had parted company years ago. His tall, dark, and handsome serenity fooled many a young female. Thinking he could be the Latin exotic, they cried with boredom when he drawled out Southernisms and preferred chasing deer to skirt. "Kids been diving illegally in the first cave area. Said they saw the body of a woman down there. We called in our divers, but they've been loaned out on a boating accident case on the Ochlockonee River. We need somebody to go down there and, at least, tell us what's there. You game?" He stared, unblinking, at me with dark marble eyes. His white shirt collar fit tight against the olive skin on his neck. The crispness of his entire garb made me wonder if he ironed before he answered a call.

"First cave? I can probably dive without equipment and make a sight identity if that's all you want." I had done things like this many times in the past. For a fee, of course. The county sheriff's department has me on their roster of certified back-up divers. My daddy taught me the basics at the edge of Fogarty Spring, then I continued with lessons and diving groups all through high school and college. When I joined the linguistics department as an associate professor, I met the archeology department—or rather Harry MacAllister, archeologist. With him, I had explored every cave in these springs, and I knew the danger.

"When you're ready," Tony Amado nodded.

I took off for the bathhouse where I changed into my bathing suit. On the way to the far end of the dock, I yelled for Tony to get someone to unload the equipment, just in case.

Standing at the edge of the boat dock I could see straight down into clear water. Farther back, water grass, that long-stemmed dark-green stuff that hides tadpoles and gators alike, blocked the view. But here, the bottom dropped suddenly to great depths. The white limestone looked inviting, unpolluted, like a huge swimming pool. Only the water stays around seventy degrees year round, colder at greater depths. It feels like a bucket of ice cubes at first, takes your breath away.

The first cave entrance bore straight down then veered off to the right. From the dock, it seemed a shadow of the tall cypress trees, but I knew it led back into a deep hole where mastodon skeletons had been found. Aiming in that direction, I dived in head first. Taking the water like this was easier than slipping in one body part at a time. After a full shock, I adjusted and headed straight for the cave opening. I could still hold my breath for three minutes if I needed to.

When I reached one side of the opening, I touched my fingertips to the rough wall to steady my view into the hole. Not too far back, the interior darkened. But just before that darkness, I saw a waving motion, something white. Moving closer, I found myself looking straight down on the top of somebody's head, somebody with gray hair. Unable to hold my breath any longer, I swam to the top and climbed the dock ladder.

"Something's down there all right, and it could be a human body. I need the tank to get a good look. You got an underwater camera on you?"

"No, but I'll bet the hotel has one." Tony helped me with the tank. "Loman get up there and see what they got," he yelled without turning to his deputy.

"There's a current down there that wants to push me all kinds of ways," I said as I squeezed water from my hair.

"You don't have to go, Luanne. You know that." Tony put his hands on his hips and spoke to the dock.

"You always say that! Are you covering your bureaucratic ass again?"

He tossed the flippers at my feet without an answer. I could see Loman near the hotel door, motioning to some preteen to go running with a camera. Good! I hated to be the only witness to something like this.

"Boss said there's only two-three pictures left in the camera, but it works real good." The kid stood wide-eyed in front of me. I must have appeared to him a comic book Amazon in flippers, tank, hoses, and mask.

Squatting at the edge of the dock, I pushed over backwards into waters that felt like the Arctic and headed for the opening once again. This time I went straight through the hole, past the white hair, treading water about five feet in front of the object.

But it wasn't an object. It was an old lady. White hair, girdle, stockings that were half unsnapped, a bra that had come loose on one side. Something strange about that side of her. Her plump arms outstretched, lots of brown liver spots. Something tied to

17

her wrist, something in a plastic bag. I moved closer, but not close enough to touch, and could swear it was a Bible waving off a small rope tied around the bluing flesh just under her palm.

I avoided looking at the face until last. This was the hard part, the human part. It had puffed up with water or death or whatever makes people's faces puff up. Her mouth and eyes, wide open, magnified inside the plastic bag that covered her head. Someone had used her glasses string to secure it around her neck. The glasses still there, bobbed at her chin. The top of the bag had been ripped and her white hair flowed out, waving back and forth in the water like a mermaid signaling her sailor-lover one last time.

When I realized I had been staring at this sight for too long, I took the camera and finished the film—three shots: the head, the arm with the Bible, and a full body photo. MacAllister had trained me well.

Topside, I handed Amado the camera as I removed the scuba gear. "You've definitely got a crime here. These pictures will shock even you. And I didn't bother to attach direction lines. Just dive straight into the opening, and there she is."

"You know we appreciate it." Tony frowned at the camera, then pretended to shake off the water.

"Yeah. And thanks for the swim." I wanted to kick his creased trousers right into the water. Nobody had a right to stay so cool in this heat, not with an old lady's corpse hanging around just below your feet.

CHAPTER TWO

I sat on the dock where the sun would dry my suit and watched the curious up near the hotel. Cop cars and men in suits on the dock brought a few tourists and workers onto the lawn where they batted gnats and scratched mosquito bites. I could smell the decaying jungle material in the shoreline black sand each time a breeze blew in my direction—swamp smell.

Tony spoke to Loman, his frustration manifesting itself in a stacatto tone and constant pacing across the floating dock. "The divers can't get here until dark, and they'd rather wait until dawn to see what's down there."

Loman swayed with the slight movement under his feet and tried to catch himself on some imaginary handle every once in a while. His response amounted to a heavy outward breath.

"You're going to have to find a place to get these developed in a hurry," said Tony. "I need to see what's down there now." He handed over the underwater camera to Loman who headed for a marked patrol car.

"Ever hear from MacAllister?" Tony borrowed a step stool from one of the glass bottom boat pilots and sat next to me.

"Why should I hear from him? He decided to chase some blond tail into the desert. He doesn't report to me." In spite of myself, I felt a bitter taste at the back of my tongue.

"I didn't expect that to last. Still don't think it will." He pulled out a pocket knife and cleaned his already spotless nails with the blade.

"Well, maybe it won't, but I'm not the type men come running back to. Unforgiving and all that."

Tony remained quiet for a few moments, long enough for me to mentally dredge up the last twelve months of my life. I had spent the summer months in the Keys with the fabulous Harry MacAllister, man of brilliant mind and sexy sinews. We had shared a houseboat and a diving venture to look at some sunken pyramid formations near the islands. We shared our expertise as well as our bodies, and our evenings in the bars, listening to local writers and artists and conquests of gay men. When the fall semester began, she came into the picture—a graduate student whose archeological delights rested in dry, dusty areas like the Arizona desert. When she received a research grant, she also found an opening for a guest lecturer. Harry applied for leave and off they went. I got a message on my machine. "I should have talked to you sooner, but this is an opportunity I can't pass up." Yeah, which opportunity are you talking about, Harry? Then Daddy died and left me with bits and pieces of property all over north Florida, including three bait and tackle shops along the Gulf.

"How come you moved into that old house, Luanne?" Tony practiced his cop's talent of looking bland and disinterested while asking the most emotional question he could formulate.

"It's my family home, where I spent a lot of my childhood days." No gray boards and leaking ceilings back then. White-latticed balconies and a newly screened porch with cane-back rockers, flowered cushions in the seats, flashed through my mind.

"But it must be falling down, at least that's what I hear."

"It's a project that's fixable. I've given up on Harry, and of course I can't bring Daddy back; I need something to repair."

"I hear you gave up your teaching job, too."

"Nope, took a year's leave. I sold those bait and tackle shops for a nice bundle. I can live without salary for a few months. Don't you ever get burned out on detecting?"

"I'm about down to embers now, why?"

"I've had it with phonemes and contrasting grammars and linguistic informants, not to mention Piaget and his theory of language acquisition. I need to do something manual, to beat the hell out of a few nails for a while. I need to swim these waters again before I have to give it up."

"Give what up?"

"Diving. Hell! I'm forty-five. How long will I be able to take the scuba gear and go down to great depths?"

"You've got a long time yet. Lots of men in their eighties still dive."

"Yeah, well, there's no guarantee I'll be able to. I'm going to do it lots of times this year."

Tony looked off into the sky which was beginning to do its afternoon rumble. "I have to close down the park, but looks like it won't matter. Going to start lightning bad in a few minutes."

Uniformed cops yellow taped the entrance to the boat tours and the swimming area. Disgruntled swimmers dragged screaming kids and inflated floats up the hill to the bathhouse. Tony placed a guard inside the ticket booth and two more inside marked cars. It would be a long mosquito-bite night with windows rolled down. The rest of us headed for the hotel.

A novelty in this part of the world, the Palmetto Hotel's lobby sports a decorative ceiling of carved and painted beams, a walk-in stone fireplace, real marble floors, and a giant stuffed alligator in a glass box. Heavy iron checker tables, with four-inch

21

marble squares to play the game, grace the room. Off the lobby, a classy restaurant with white tablecloths and a bank of glass windows allows a panoramic view of the springs. Waitresses in starched black-and-white roll out carts of Southern food: fried chicken, pork chops, spoon bread, fried okra, black-eyed peas, and pecan pie. The hotel, once a tax write-off and a hide-a-way for a big Northern company, now belongs to the state, serving as a local haunt for the geriatric set.

The officers headed for the comfortable sofas and the checkers tables. I headed for the ladies' room to change into my smelly shorts and top. A lot of enforcing the law around here means a waiting game for the right equipment to arrive—in this case, the professional divers.

As I returned to the lobby, Loman rushed through the front door. "Got a one-hour place to do these," he wheezed and brushed his sweaty forehead with a shirt sleeve. "Had to show him my badge since he didn't want to do this kind of film. Pictures came out fine." He handed the package to Tony then went in search of iced tea in the dining room. I suspected he really wanted a beer.

"Lots of grass, catfish, some baby gators—okay, here! Is this what you saw?" Tony handed me one of my three photos, the closeup of the old lady's face.

"That's it. You know her?"

"Doesn't look like anybody I've seen lately. I'll get Loman to find out if any old ladies have gone missing." He stopped to look at each of the three pictures. He didn't wince even once. I knew Tony had a grandmother somewhere. He might have been thinking about her, but you'd never know it.

Outside, lightning flashed close, the noise slamming into the glass windows. Everyone jumped, then laughed nervously. Even if the divers showed up, no way would they go into the water until this storm passed. I wanted to get home before the downpour, because if those puddles got any worse, I wouldn't make it at all. When I snatched up my car keys, Tony held up his hand.

"You need to stay around. I'll see to it you get a room in the hotel if I have to. The other divers may need you."

"You going to buy me some clothes, too? All I've got are these dirty things and my swimming suit."

"The shop's over there. You've got credit here, don't you?" He smiled slightly.

We sat around the lobby until the sky grew dark from the storm. Rain pounded against the giant windows, making the air-conditioning even colder. Tony had built a tower with marble checkers when a clerk leaned over the counter and called his name, the phone receiver in one hand.

When Tony returned from the call, his slightly furrowed brow revealed disappointment. "Divers can't get away right now. This case on the Ochlockonee is pretty bad, and they've had a storm there, too. We'll meet them here first thing in the morning." He made the announcement and appointed some guards to replace the others. The whole bunch left.

There I stood, in sweaty shorts in the middle of a fancy lobby in a summer downpour that would have blocked my view out the windshield even if it didn't trap my car. It was dark; dinner lured me to the dining room, and I had plastic. I hurried to the hotel shop, bought a pair of jogging pants, a tee shirt, a tooth-brush and toothpaste. Then I checked into one of the rooms.

Somewhat presentable, I returned to the dining room for a sumptuous Southern meal—fried pork chops, hopping john, collards, and corn bread. Why not? I had fed on salads and steamed fish for days. My own kitchen was too hot and too primitive to spend much time there.

The rain finally stopped around ten. I could have driven home, but I wanted comfort, the kind you got when other people did the cooking and cleaning, if for just one night. I took a seat on the glassed-in porch where I watched a lone squirrel trek across the brick patio and run up a tree. Beyond the tree, it was too dark to see the glass bottom boats and the ticket office where the guard kept watch over an old lady's watery grave. Across the patio, I could barely see a dock light in the distance. Warm mist sat on top of singing crickets and frogs. Occasionally, something would break a limb or crush a leaf, but nothing revealed itself—probably deer rummaging around after the rain.

Later, in the antique brass bed that stood high off the marble floor, my mind jumped about like a grasshopper on hot pavement. Something about that woman's chest. One side of it just wasn't there—a scar. Then it hit me: a mastectomy, of course!

I lay there staring at the fancy ceiling with its early Florida scenes. A Spanish galleon anchored off shore, and a Seminole maiden dressed in a colorful frock waded into the waves to offer the armored conquistadors in small boats—what? I couldn't make out the food products in her basket. *The old lady had a scar about seven inches long. Her skin around the scar was lumpy and slightly discolored. The bra on that side had been floating freely. Probably had a prosthesis that slipped away when she hit the water. What held her down in that current?* I made out some corn and melons in the Indian maiden's basket and tire-size flowers dropping to the ground in front of her. The poor girl had no idea what those Spaniards had in mind for her.

24

In the dining room, I ate the breakfast of my dreams: country bacon, cheese grits, eggs scrambled in milk, and cane syrup on buttered biscuits. From my window table, I watched the trucks and patrol cars drive up to the dock. As promised, Amado had shut down the park. As soon as I had finished the last of my coffee, I saw the important van drive up, a bulging white thing that housed all the underwater crime scene equipment. Three men stood to the side and pulled on black wet suits. Grabbing their tanks and flippers, they headed for the dock. Two other men walked behind them with a large box. I wanted to see this.

Tony, neatly pressed and creased, caught sight of me coming down the bricks used for a walkway and waved me toward him. Loman, a dress suit surrounded by rubber ones, briefed the divers with the pictures I took yesterday.

"Where exactly is this cave?" one of the divers asked. None of the three had been down in this particular spring. I pointed to the permanent shadow, then told them how to use the sides to hold themselves in these currents.

"It's tricky down there. If you relax, you'll move away pretty quickly. I think the body is tethered somehow. It wasn't moving."

The divers pushed over backwards, then silently headed for the depths. Tony paced, his patience for the unseeable growing thin. The rest of the forensics people stood near the glass bottom boats, waiting to bag anything the woman had on her. She would be a spectacle on this dock in bright sunlight. Her bloated body washed clean in the cold water, she would lie in full view of nearly twenty males who would grope, poke, and pull at her until they found who placed her in such an undignified position in the first place.

The divers took too long. By now they should have located her, then sent for a retrieving cage. I had visions of them running into trouble, of the current catching one and bashing him against the limestone wall, or pushing him into a side hole so that he became disoriented and couldn't get out. It had happened many times in these underwater holes, even to experienced divers.

A black head bobbed at the surface, then another, and finally all three men held onto the edge of the dock.

"We couldn't find her. There's no body down there." They pulled off their tanks and handed them to assistants. "You sure about the cave?"

I nodded. "There has to be—you saw the pictures." I looked at Tony—no expression. "I believe some teenage boys saw it yesterday," I said, glaring at him for not answering.

"Then maybe you ought to find those boys. Maybe they moved it," one diver called out from the water.

"In the night?" I yelled back.

"Why not? Divers have lights, and the water is totally clear down there."

"You didn't even see any evidence of her?" Tony spoke to the diver but looked at me.

"Checked the wall real good, even took some pictures myself. We didn't see a thing."

The divers climbed aboard the dock and unzipped their suit tops, letting them hang from the crotch. One, in his fifties, balding, rugged, with a lined face, made me glad to see he was still at it.

"I'm going back down. Help me get my gear." I moved toward the Honda.

"Is this wise?" Tony never turned around to hear an answer.

At the bathhouse once again, I wrestled into my suit, then headed for the dock. I placed the tank on my back, eased over the side, and swam for the cave. The cold current waved around me

26

as I braced myself against the wall. I stared at the white spot where yesterday I had seen a gross sight. Today, it was pristine. Not a single hole in the stone, not a plastic bag, not the hint of an old lady. I looked below me. Maybe the current pulled her down then rushed her into one of the other holes, holes too deep to search without special equipment and buddies. No gator would dive this deep. Unless she somehow floated to the shallows, I knew no animal predator had taken the body away.

Back on the dock, I asked questions that no one could answer, including what the guards saw during the night. They had neither seen nor heard anything.

The old lady had simply vanished.

CHAPTER THREE

Grilling from a bunch of male cops who know damned well they already had the truth might be a lesson in humility. But I've long since stopped feeling humble in the presence of anyone whose patience gave out. I went home, but not before leaving Tony with the word that he'd have to get on his knees and beg if he ever intended to use me in one of his cases again.

Since they didn't know what else to do, they questioned my mind: Was I sure there was a body down there? Why didn't I attach direction lines? Did I really take those pictures? Damn! How could anyone take pictures like that just to fool a bunch of cops—and on the spur of the moment?

I drove full speed over the rutted road, hitting the puddles full blast. Muddy water splattered everywhere, but a good car washing would be my battering ram for the afternoon. My last words to Tony were "I'm going back into my swamp and never come out again. Don't call me!" He threw up his hands, took a deep breath, and stalked off to the divers who had moved away from our confrontation. He would insist they go under again to explore all the caves, then swim along the shoreline of the entire spring to search for any sign of body removal.

The caves had tricky currents and the shoreline was a haven for snakes and storage places for gator food. Damn critters kill a deer, then let it soak in shallow water, tenderizing the meat. A juicy diver would get the same treatment. The cops didn't know the territory like I did, but they did know the dangers. They would need me again. The only person who knew those caves better than me was MacAllister, and he was in Arizona.

When I finally pulled into my yard—mowed wild grass under oak trees—the weather decided I needed a break and began to drizzle, then pour in buckets. The Honda would shine squeaky clean in this natural washing. Later, I would pull it under the posts and roof that served as a carport on the side of the house.

Dragging my new clothes with me, I made a run for the front door and trudged upstairs, the old boards threatening to crack with every footstep. At the top, I dodged a hole then jumped over a missing step. I had been working here when Pasquin came to me with the summons.

Pasquin, a nosy old fellow, had been here last night to find out what happened. He'd be back again soon. The porch chairs turned on their fronts told me this. It protected the seats from a blowing rain, he said. He didn't want to sit in wet chairs or have to come inside.

The rain hit the tin roof like buckshot from a hundred guns just overhead. I rushed into the big room—what I hoped would become the master bedroom—to see about leaks. I had placed some heavy plastic over the side of the roof that would be repaired as soon as Bailey Construction could get its act together. A falling-down house in the middle of the swamp wasn't one of their priorities.

Things seemed okay, and I started toward the small room on the other side of the upstairs, the one I slept in temporarily. On the landing I heard the boards, the stairs groaning as someone came toward me. The hair on my neck froze straight up in spite of the humidity.

"Just me, ma'am," Pasquin's face looked up at me, his hat over his chest. "I knocked, but in this rain, guess you didn't hear. Then, ma'am, you left the door ajar. Did you know that? Gon' have some unwelcome visitor in here one day if you keep that up."

"Animal or human?"

"Could be either one—panther, snake, bear, maybe even a little deer. Then again, it might be that creature they done filmed from around here." He stood on the middle stair and grinned up at me. He referred to a B-grade horror movie filmed around here in the fifties. Locals still talk about the handsome young diver who played a half-fish, half-wolf creature, and it's on the boat tour recital list.

I laughed. "Something like that will fall right through those stairs, and you will, too, if you aren't careful. I'll be down in a minute, Pasquin."

He took my hint and moved back into the living room. I could see him take my favorite chair by the big window that faced the screen porch. For a moment I watched him gaze toward the river, and I remembered when Daddy died. I had gone through my mother's old trunk where I found some diaries of her years during the war. With Daddy away, she took solace in a neighbor nearly twenty years her senior—Pasquin. The old pictures showed him a dashing fellow, the kind who would know how to charm a lonely war bride on a humid Florida night. It gnawed at me often, so much that I wondered if Daddy really was my daddy, that maybe Pasquin.... I shook myself. Life's little nagging thoughts again. Get over it!

Changed into clean togs, I joined Pasquin in some iced tea and crackers. We dripped sweat since I didn't have an air conditioner to blow a cold streak through my house. Every time I left home, I had to close all the windows in case a rain came up. While here, I could open up the window near Pasquin's seat, because the porch roof protected it from the rain. It, and a large electric fan, were the only sources of cool I had.

"Anything worth talking about?" Pasquin winked at me.

"Found a body in a cave. No one knows who she is. Once I did the discovery work for them, the cops weren't interested in anything else I had to say." I deliberately avoided talking about the bizarre appearance of the lady, her age and her subsequent disappearance.

"Fools drown in those caves every year. Bet half of them are never found, just get caught in a current and washed on down the river or on down the cave. Bet there's a pile of old bones in the bottom of those caves."

"Yeah. But who's found the bottom?" I sipped on the cold liquid.

"Hah! Who'd want to? If you found the bottom, it'd be 'cause your bones were about to get deposited in the same spot."

We sat in silence as Southern people always have, looking at and listening to the rain, our tea glasses making wet rings on the tables. There was no hurry to say anything. I felt my anger subside, the peace of nature overcome me. When I heard a large bullfrog croak near the porch, I laughed and knew the rain would be over soon.

"I got a favor to ask you, ma'am." Pasquin leaned forward, his elbows resting on his knees, tea glass in one hand, hat in the other. "One of my relatives done went and had a heart attack. She is supposed to have left me a little of her 'state. Thought I better go on over to the funeral. Can't get there in the boat. Maybe you'd drive me—if you wasn't too busy?"

Pasquin, from the old school of just about everything, had learned to drive long before licensing became popular, but when he got a ticket for hitting a parked van, the cops said no more car. He bought himself a nice new motor boat instead. It took him up and down the river to visit old friends and to the meat and produce store near the river bank in Fogarty Spring. He never minded the loss of his car.

"When is it?"

"Sunday—seems they plan to combine the service with the regular Sunday preaching. Over to the Spring Baptist."

"Pasquin, for some reason I could have sworn you were Catholic."

"Am, but never told much of anybody. Catholics rare as elephants 'round here. Some of the people in the old days wouldn't hear of it—called it idol worship. Huh! At least the old priest don't go yelling at everybody about fornication. All that stuff just 'rouses the libido of young kids." He laughed quietly. "Tit-till-lating!"

"Okay. I'll drive you. Time?"

He explained that we'd have to start out at ten-thirty to get there for the viewing and speaking to relatives and such. I could sit in the car and wait if I wanted.

"No, Pasquin. I'll go with you. You've done a lot for me. Won't hurt me to sit through a sermon anyhow."

"My cousin would thank you if she could. Lordy, lying there in a casket. Don't like them things. She's younger than me, too." He paused, then sighed. "I still remember that curly top of hair that bounced all over her head just after her mama washed it. Prettiest little imp you done saw. Never could see why she didn't marry."

An uneasy quiet filled the room. I hadn't married either, and

32

Pasquin mentioned it often. I once exploded into something like mind your own business for a change. He had remained silent about it nearly a month.

The rain stopped almost as suddenly as it had started. A few drops still fell from the tin roof, and the bullfrog had set up an aria of croaking. Pasquin thanked me, then rose to leave. "I'll knock that bullfrog away for you. Drive you crazy, them things." He held the screen door so it wouldn't slam, then slowly climbed down the steps.

I smiled as he stopped, swung one leg back, then forward, and felt sorry for the fat bullfrog, its dignity spent on a rainy afternoon.

"You lock that screen, hear?" He waved his hat as he faded into the forest.

As soon as he was out of sight, I regretted my promise. Two things I just couldn't stand—church and funerals—and I had agreed to go to both. Curiosity about Pasquin's family got the best of me, not knowing if they spoke the same Cajun dialect or maybe had simply become Southern Baptists and voted Republican. Of course, my genetic suspicions got the best of me, too. Just in case he really was my father, I needed to meet his people, didn't I?

Pounding rain woke me again in the middle of the night, and I began to worry that I wouldn't be able to get the Honda through the mud to take Pasquin to the funeral. Funny how worries like this magnify themselves in darkness. I switched on the table lamp and picked up a book on remoisturizing old boards. It didn't do much to put me asleep, just made my mind search for more creative things. I looked up at the ceiling. No Seminole girl-

Spanish conquistador stuff here. The narrow boards had gaps between them from years of settling, but I had painted them a nice ivory and they looked gentle, almost. I planned to get some lace curtains; on a balmy night, they would blow across the twin bed in this room. That's what I remember most about this house. Afternoons and early evenings, lying across my quilt-topped bed, lace curtains blowing over me, reading *Jane Eyre*. Or maybe it was Nancy Drew.

There were nights when my mother read to me. She sat in a rocker next to the bed. She always wore a yellow robe with white slippers. Her hair would be down after a day of wearing it at the nape of her neck in a bun. She brushed it a lot at night, then came in here with me. Her soft voice, "Once upon a time..." I tried to hold the memory, but it always escaped and turned into a funeral.

"Take a last look, child." Those were the only words I can remember coming from my old grandfather. His daughter—my mother—had died of cancer in this very house. Old and frail, he went the winter after that. I had to go to another funeral.

"Take a last look, child." At what? A mannequin with a plastic face inside a silky box? It wasn't really my mother.

"Place a flower inside, dear." Some lady whispered and handed me a rose. I touched one of the thorns, deliberately hurting myself. Then, I stood on tiptoe and placed the rose on my mother's arm, but I didn't let go. I pressed that thorn hard into her arm. Nothing happened. I pressed harder. She didn't wake up, but I could hear the lady gasping behind me. Then my daddy's big hands came around and gently took the flower away from me. He placed it on Mother's chest and led me away.

We kept on living here until Daddy could stand it no longer. He did well in his bait and tackle stores, and moved us to a brick house in Tallahassee where I went to school. But this place was always my solitude, and I returned often, just to sit on the old boards and listen to the sounds of the swamp, to wade around the edges of the river, swim in the springs.

A mosquito brought me back to the present. He buzzed around my head, looking for a landing place to attack. I tried to swat him with my book but he flew to the ceiling. Standing on the bed, I waited until he sat perfectly still, then squashed him flat against the new ivory paint. Blood spattered. He had bitten me somewhere. Then I remembered it was the female mosquito that sucked blood. I called it a *ho-dyke* and headed for the ancient bathroom near the landing. Mentally cursing myself for dirtying the ceiling, I stopped dead at the first creak—then another. From where I stood, I couldn't see past the middle of the stairs. The creaking stopped. I took off for the bathroom and grabbed a flashlight from under the sink. It came in handy every time there was a power outage. I stood up against the wall and switched it on, aiming it at the bottom of the stairs. Neon eyes froze, and two more behind those. Two gray raccoons sat on the second step, staring at me. I lifted the light toward the front door. The screen lay open like a giant peeled scab, but the latch was secure. Grabbing hold of the toilet plunger, I hit the steps with it until the loud sucking sounds forced the animals to retreat through the hole they had made. In spite of the heat, I closed the solid door.

Downstairs, I stood on the porch for a moment. Gazing across the yard, the trees, the swamp grass, and toward the river, I heard a putt-putt in the distance and saw a small light move away from me, growing smaller as a midnight boat wound with the river.

CHAPTER FOUR

The funeral started late. And that was a good thing. It took us an hour of maneuvering around deep puddles to get to the main road. Once, Pasquin had to get out and lay pine needles across a puddle where the road shoulder had eroded. He took off his shirt, tie and coat, rolled up his pants legs and chucked the socks and shoes to do it. Afterwards, we stopped near a stream so he could wash the mud off his feet and ankles.

We pulled into the parking area under some tall pines. A congress of elderly women in flower-print dresses, their hair shining like white bunny tails, surrounded the wood-frame church steps. A few old men huddled together under a spreading oak, telling off-color jokes about things they hadn't done in years. They all turned around when Pasquin and I emerged from the Honda.

We stood and stared at the crowd, and they at us, for a few moments until the preacher came forward to greet Pasquin.

"Welcome to our church, brother. You are Dorian Pasquin, I assume?"

"Sure am, sir. Is it time to begin the funeral?"

"Yessir. We were holding it up. Thought you and your—ahem—wife might like to view the deceased before the others come inside."

Pasquin looked at me and winked, then took my arm. We

followed the preacher up the cement steps. Inside, I almost retched. The overwhelming smell of flowers, the cleaning liquid used by the ladies of the circle, and the long mahogany coffin sitting directly ahead hit me with a wave of nausea. I swallowed hard and followed Pasquin to the front, passing shiny wooden pews with hymnals. The preacher stopped in front of the half-open casket.

"She looks just like she did last Sunday when she attended services for the last time. Heart attack," he whispered gently, "took her Wednesday morning. A neighbor lady found her that evening. Doctors say she didn't suffer at all, just went suddenly to the Lord. Mr. Pasquin." He stepped aside. I stood a few feet back, not wanting to see anything. Funny how I could look at that dead woman in the spring, but I sure didn't want to see this one in a coffin.

Before I could sit down and pretend to pray, the preacher took my arm gently and pulled me forward. The coffin half-lid, the part over the face and upper body, stood open. I saw white hair neatly spread out over a light-purple satin pillow, a slightly puffy face on which someone had brushed rouge and lipstick, and arms crossed over a chest. She wore a flowered dress just like those standing around outside. Her forearms and hands had the liver spots of old age. She held a bouquet of violets in her hands.

I stared. All I could see was white hair floating in the current of spring water, of wide-open eyes and mouth, of liver spots on arms. I had seen this woman in the spring—this very woman. Gasping, I staggered backward slightly and the preacher grabbed me around the waist.

"Oh, dear, not used to this sort of thing, are you?"

"Luanne, what's the matter?" Pasquin helped the preacher seat me in a pew.

"Pasquin, would you mind terribly if I didn't stay? I don't feel well. It's too much of a reminder of other funerals I've been

37

to," I lied.

Pasquin looked at the preacher. "Her daddy passed a few months ago. Mama died when she was just a young thing."

The preacher nodded and frowned concern for me. Pasquin pulled me up and said, "You go on home, Luanne. I know a few people out there who will take me back to the house. I'll see you there."

I stayed in a little room off the side of the pulpit until most of the people had come inside the church, then I made fast tracks to the Honda. I had to get to Tony Amado before burial took place. Assuming he'd be at the springs, I headed in that direction.

"She's what?" Tony, agitated enough to make his divers look down and smile, leaned into my face. "How the hell can a woman who's been in water appear 'natural' in an open casket?"

"I'm telling you, Tony, it's the same woman. Bring those pictures and take a look for yourself. If you hurry, you can see her at the church. Otherwise, you'll have to make that preacher open the casket before he buries her."

He stared at the sky and then at his feet for a few minutes, his only facial expression a grinding of the lower jaw against the upper. The divers, Loman, and a couple of uniformed guys watched in silence.

"All right! Loman give me those pictures. Stay here and supervise this search. And you fellows," he turned to the divers, "don't drown!"

I pulled into the churchyard just as the first of the elderly mourners came through the front door. I scooted down at first, then sneaked into the same pulpit room I had been in before. Tony had parked behind my car, and I thought he would follow my lead. Not Tony. He marched right in the front door.

Pasquin and three others sat on the front pew, their heads slightly bowed. The preacher stood behind the casket, nodding to people as they filed past the old lady. Some dabbed at their eyes, but most took a quick glance, then hurried on, as though too much of a reminder of their own fate. Taking advantage of all the walking around, I sneaked into the pew next to one of the three men. Pasquin looked toward me, whispered something to the man next to him, then all three scooted up so I could sit next to him.

"This is your relative, Pasquin. Who is she?" I whispered.

"Why, Carmina Twiggins. I thought you knew that." He looked at me, a little surprised at my breathless words.

"No! You never said her name, just that she's a relative, a cousin, you said."

"Yes, second cousin on my father's side, why?"

"And she died of a heart attack?"

"That's what they told me. Why?"

Our whispering attracted the ears of the three men on the pew. I turned sideways, my back to them. "See that man going toward the preacher? That's sheriff's detective Amado. Your cousin looks just like the woman we found in the spring."

"She drowned?" Pasquin's whisper changed to full voice. Faces turned around to stare at him.

I patted his hand and nodded toward the preacher who listened to Tony tell him he needed to compare the deceased to some pictures. At first the preacher shook his head, but when Tony showed him the photos of the woman in the spring, he stepped away to give him a better view. After looking from photo to corpse a few times, Tony invited the preacher to make the same comparison. His sweaty forehead revealed his answer. Tony glanced at me and nodded.

Outside, Tony cornered the hearse driver and another mortuary official. I approached them just in time to hear him say, "You're not burying her now. This is a police case. Take the body back to your mortuary and tell your boss to stand by."

Pasquin hurried outside. "The preacher told everyone to go home, that the family had encountered a little problem with burial. Tongues will be waggin' tonight!"

Tony headed for his car. "The body will be at Palmetto in the only funeral home there. Mr. Pasquin, I expect you to be right behind me."

Two cars sped away as nearly thirty-five bewildered mourners looked after us. I stayed dangerously close on Tony's tail all the way to Palmetto. We pulled up in front of an antebellum mansion, refurbished to house the dead.

Inside, thick burgundy curtains hung over windows, walls, and maybe doors. Who could tell? The whole building seemed draped to look like a coffin, maybe a reminder that the living aren't so different from the dead after all. Pasquin and I stood outside the office while Tony went inside to tell the funeral home director he would have to undo a lot of what he had just done.

"'Tis bad luck to be in a place like this, Luanne. This going to take long?" Pasquin fanned himself with his hat in spite of the near freezing air conditioning. I figured a little Creole superstition had mixed with the Cajun when he crossed his forehead with his thumb.

"Depends on what we find."

Tony came out with a worried little black-suited man who prissed ahead of us to the end of a corridor. He parted some more burgundy curtains then pushed open dull, metal sliding doors right behind them. We stood in the embalming room, and I had to agree with Pasquin—this had to be bad luck. A buzzer sounded near an outside door somewhere, and the little man hurried to answer it.

"Bring her in. We'll use this table." I heard him talking to the hearse drivers.

We followed Tony through a maze of steel tables to one in the back. There was Pasquin's cousin, all gussied up in flowers—on her dress and in her hands. But she didn't look comfortable on the table. The satin pillow from the coffin was gone, causing her head to tilt backwards at an unnatural angle.

"This look like the woman in these pictures?" Tony thrust the photos in front of the undertaker's nose. The man gave him a disapproving glare for a moment, then snatched the pictures with a flair. He jerked his head back and forth, sighed and twitched in agreement.

"Yes, it does look like her. But I could swear she came in as a heart attack victim. A doctor signed the certificate."

"Check out her chest," I said.

"Her what?" Tony turned his eyes to me.

"Look at that picture in the water. She's had an operation, a breast removed. Check out the woman in the coffin."

Pasquin turned pale and faced the other direction. He even crossed himself. The undertaker waited for Tony to nod, then moved to the body and began to unbutton the dress, each button hidden in a flower design. When he got to the real flowers in her hands, he had to pry them apart and push her stiff hands aside. They ended up with the palms resting against her stomach and the fingers spread wide, pointing upward. Pasquin peeked from behind his hat. When he spied the fingers, he had to sit down.

41

"I'll have to remove the binding." The undertaker's face took on a questioning mode, hoping Tony would say there was no need.

"Just do it."

With a pair of large scissors, he cut through some white material bound around the lady's chest. I had visions of flapper days when flat chests were the rage and voluptuousness had to be hidden at the cost of comfort. For one mad moment, I hoped the lady would stand up and do the Charleston.

"See for yourself, folks." The undertaker had gently laid the ends of the cut cloth to each side. Tony looked first.

"Yeah, well, I guess this one's got two huge knockers all right. Don't look sewed on, either," said Tony. The crease danced between his eyebrows.

The men and I gazed down at large breasts whose firmness had disappeared forty years before. Without the binding, they fell stiffly to the woman's sides.

"Pasquin, can you tell us anything about your cousin?" He jumped. His perpetual leathery skin turned green.

"I know that's my cousin in there. I don't have to look again." He fanned as though the wind would remove evil spirits.

"Then why the hell does she look like this woman in the photos?" Tony's frustration peeked through at last.

Pasquin raised halfway up from his chair, took the photos and looked at them hard. "Now, my cousin had a sister. They were a year apart, but when they was growing up, they looked just like twins—dressed alike and everything. Somewhere along the line, they had a falling out over who was going to get their mama's jewelry and dishes. Carmina got the house; Delia thought she ought to have the other stuff. They just stopped talking to each other. Delia—Carmina's sister—stomped out of the house and ended up in Texas somewhere. The family pretty much forgot about her, and Carmina sure never said anything about her. Now just maybe they still looked alike when they got old. Suppose?" His whole face became a question mark.

Silence filled the room—two males and a female looked in wonderment at Pasquin. A dead female lay in indignity, her chest exposed for all to see. Tony leaned forward slightly. "Why the hell didn't you tell us this before, old man?"

"Now, here, here, sir, nobody asked me. 'sides, I just thought about it this very moment. It's been maybe forty years since I even heard the sister's name."

Tony's face reddened. Instead of exploding, he walked over to a telephone on a small metal desk and dialed a familiar number. "Sally, get me all you can on a Delia Twiggins. Probably lives in Texas somewhere." He held his hand over the receiver. "Pasquin, did she marry and change her name, and what city are we talking about?"

"Don't know neither, sir. Twiggins was their maiden name, and Carmina never married. Maybe you ought to search Carmina's house. Somewhere, she's got to have all that information."

Tony's usually cool, pale-olive skin looked sunburned now. He yelled into the phone. "And start a search warrant procedure on Carmina Twiggins' home!"

"Guess you believe me now, Tony?" I had to whisper this to him as he passed me on the way to his car.

He turned around suddenly. "I never doubted you. Harry taught me to never doubt you. He said you were about the most capable female he'd ever met." With that he got into his car and slammed the door. Pasquin and I followed him outside. He had to pull up, then turn around to avoid some bushes. To make it interesting, I stood in front of the car.

He rolled down his window. "What the hell?"

43

"This means you're going to ask me to dive with those men, right? And maybe bring Pasquin along to help with the search?"

"Get out of the way. I'll let you know. Just stay home. I want to know where to find you!" He started to leave, then slammed on brakes. "Here! Take this and use it." He held a cell phone at arm's length out the window.

When I stepped aside, he dug ruts.

CHAPTER FIVE

I paced the floorboards until I could stand it no longer. After a fitful night of seeing breastless women swimming in my dreams, I tried the cell phone to call Tony. It picked up nothing; I was out of range in this swamp. Still in my "Alligator Point" tee that I slept in, I drove the Honda across the dirt road, then a mile down the paved road before I hit a live zone.

"We checked some hospitals after we found an address in Beaumont, Texas. Delia Twiggins had a mastectomy for cancer of the breast in 1989. She left her address last week, closing out her rented apartment. No one seems to know where she went." Amado, calm now, gave me, in his natural monotone, the information his secretary had collected.

I shifted the telephone to my other ear. "She went to the bottom of the spring."

Silence. "Okay, quit the jabs. We've got a search warrant for her sister's house, though as next of kin and heir, Pasquin could take us through himself. Have to make things legal. We don't want a hassle later in court."

"Then you expect to find something?"

"I don't know what to expect. We've got the Beaumont people checking things out there. Look, what I want you to do is grab Pasquin and get him to his cousin's house within the next

45

hour. We'll meet you there."

"Gotcha! Do I get to swim with the big guys next?" I made a u-turn and headed home.

The short walk over the swamp path to Pasquin's seemed an eternity today. I dripped behind my knees, all over my clean jeans. Dodging muddy spots and sinister leaf piles, I wound through oaks and pines that grew fuzzy things on their trunks. I knew from childhood that if I pressed one of those gray balls, a little insect would crawl out. Tree cooties, we called them. I rounded a tree and ran into a family of frogs crossing from the river side to the swamp side of the forest. They paused, their rapid heartbeats throbbing against their rubber-like skin, then hopped ahead, then stopped again. I let all six cross before going on. In the distance I heard the high-pitched tone of a baby gator calling for its mama, and the mama's deep bellow in answer.

I pounded on Pasquin's front door, trying to make myself heard over his roaring air conditioner.

"My, Luanne, don't beat the thing to death." He appeared around the side of the house, grasping a shovel caked with mud.

"Sorry, I didn't know you weren't inside. We're going to your cousin's house. The police want to search the place."

He stood still, then slowly began to fan himself with his silly hat. Finally, he shrugged, leaned the shovel against the porch, and followed me back through the swamp. I could swear we met the same frog family returning to the river across the path. Pasquin hurried them along by kicking at the dirt near their pulsating bodies. Some of them wouldn't move until he actually nudged them with the toe of his shoe.

"Just got to kick some bastards hard to get them to understand," he said.

While Pasquin pointed down this paved road and that dirt one, and finally across a narrow rutted lane, then to an even narrower drive, I tried to guide the car around holes and clumps of grass that no one had bothered to cut. Some of the center grass had been mashed down by the police cars and a hearse, but nothing as small as a Honda. By the time we pulled into the yard beside Tony's black sedan and one patrol car, I was exhausted from turning a wheel without power steering.

"Your cousin lived farther back in the swamp than you do," I said.

"Family property. Owned it for generations back. It's mine now, but I got no longing to move here. 'sides, who would I get for a driver way back here?" He grinned at me like a satisfied cat, then made a dash for the wrap-around porch. It had just begun to rain.

"Finally," said a grumpy Tony. His puffy eyes said he'd been up all night, but his clothes still had that recently pressed shine. When the rain started to come down harder, he glanced up at the ceiling with a scowl. "Let's get going. Mr. Pasquin, I'm looking for things that point to your other cousin, the one in Texas. I want to know if she was here, if any papers can tell us her background. And, of course, photos. Before we tear this place apart, do you have any idea where stuff like that would be?"

"Big house, sir. Woman like that could keep things almost anywhere, especially since she's lived here all her natural life. Now I got asked over for ice tea and widow company lots of times, but nobody said I could go snooping around. I know where the cognac is, though. Had to mix a little in the tea in order to join in the conversation."

"Okay, let's do it." Tony ignored Pasquin's comments and waved to the two men huddled away from the blowing rain. "Try not to disturb order too much. Mr. Pasquin, I'll work alongside you."

I tried to make myself invisible from Tony by wandering in and out of rooms. I sized up the place as a typical Southern home, occupied for seventy-plus years by one woman—crocheted doilies everywhere, fluffy curtains, matching kitchen canisters, nice English tea set on a tea cart, beautiful heirloom china and silver, homemade quilts on the upstairs beds, round framed pictures of generations of family members. A few modern things like a small television set with earphones sat in what appeared to be the woman's own bedroom. In another bedroom, a multi-band radio that looked almost brand-new sat next to a large recliner. I switched on the radio.

An announcer called baseball moves from a game in Ohio. While it played, I opened the closet door. Men's flannel shirts stared back at me. I heard the announcer say, "This is your all-sports station..."

All sports? Not too many women Carmina's age listen to an all-sports station. I looked back at the flannel shirts. Many women down South do wear men's flannel shirts in the winter time. I began to see flannel shirts and all-sports radio stations together, and they didn't add up to sweet, old Carmina Twiggins. I would have to speak to Mr. touchy Tony Amado, after all.

Pasquin fanned himself in the stifling room. Carmina's power had been cut off, leaving us without air-conditioning. "Don't recall her having interest in any kind of sport, except swimming in the springs. I 'member all us kids stripping down to underwear and flying into that clear water. Little Carmina's lips would blue up from the cold. Come to think of it, so did Delia's." His eyes teared, from memories or humidity, I couldn't tell.

"Does look like someone else stayed here. Look at this." Tony shoved a small box of tie tacks and baseball cards in front of Pasquin's eyes.

"My, my. You think my cousin had a man-friend at her age?"

"And these." Tony stood before a pulled-out drawer, looking down at white shirts still in their packages. "Unless your cousin was a cross dresser, sir, a male is living here."

Suddenly, one of Tony's men called from the other end of the hall. Tony pushed us out ahead of him and closed the door, muttering something about a more thorough search.

In a parlor that opened onto the kitchen, the deputy pointed toward the back of a wooden easy chair, the kind that is large and full of pillows. "Look at this, sir. There's a chip here, recently made, and something that looks like blood on it." We leaned over in unison. Tony stood his ground and gave us a disgusted look. We backed away.

"Get the crime scene people out here." He snapped and pushed Pasquin and me to the front porch. He ordered us to let him know when the crime scene van arrived.

On the front porch, we had pulled two rockers up to a small round table, and sat close to the wall to keep dry when Tony deposited three albums in Pasquin's lap.

"We found these," he said.

"Gon' to get wet out here, sir." Pasquin raised them to the table.

Tony motioned for us to follow him inside. "Sit here, but

don't wander." He pointed to the kitchen table and a couple of plain wooden chairs whose seat cushions had been removed.

Pasquin opened the first album and loose photos fell to the floor. I picked them up. Yellowed sepia showed grim women in high-collared, long-sleeved dresses that scraped the floor. One woman revealed a shoe that must have buttoned above the ankle. They stood on a porch, probably the one on this house. I could feel the strangle of humidity under layers of clothes in a Florida summer.

"Looks like a few missing here. Maybe the glue just wore off and they're loose." Pasquin kept flipping through pages. "Here's me!" He grinned, then pulled the picture out of its black triangular holders. He showed me three boys in underwear used as swim suits, their wet hair slicked back. "Been swimming in the river. That's my other cousins on the other side of the family. Dead now. But we did have some fun back then. Scared of nothing— not water snakes, gators, nothing."

"Any grudges crop up in your family, Pasquin?" I asked.

"Grudges all over the place. Cajun family marries into regular Protestant family, you got grudges all right. Some were right funny. You know one time my mama took whole bunches of my daddy's family to one of them 'dinner-on-the-ground' things over at the Baptist church. Soon as everybody finished serving themselves, my daddy's friends got out the fiddles and started into singing and dancing the Cajun. Baptists squawked something awful about that! And, Carmina, well she was mostly Baptist, but the Cajun fellows got to her, pulled her into the dance along with them. I still teased her about that dancing. Probably never did another jig in her life." He chuckled for a while, remembering little incidents at the dinner-turned-Cajun party that remained offensive to the Baptists for years. "Yep, Mama never forgave Daddy for that day."

"Most of the Cajuns died out, didn't they?"

"Died out or moved away to the Louisianne. 'Course, there's me and some others still around here, but not enough to say we have a community. Hell, we could never get up a party like that again."

We continued through the albums, almost forgetting our real task of finding Delia's pictures. When Pasquin came to the third album, he gave a whoop. "Most stuff is gone from here!" He pointed to pages of faded squares and brittle black holders, but no photographs. "Here's a few of Carmina and her ladies group. They met off and on at the church, but where are all the others?"

Tony came into the kitchen with a handful of photographs. He spread them over the table with a gloved hand. The bent corners made them appear to be torn from the album.

"Where'd you find these?" Pasquin asked.

"In the corner over there." Tony nodded over his shoulder. "Any of Delia?"

"This—and this, and—oh my!" Pasquin pointed without touching the old family photos. Scenes of smiling children in lace dresses and frowning old ladies with high collars—all slashed with angry streaks from a modern ball point pen.

"You've got a problem here, detective," I said.

"Got lots of problems, here." Pasquin leaned back and sighed. "Disgusting! Who done this to this lady?" He waved his hands across the pictures like a magician who wanted them invisible.

"That's all for you guys until we get these dusted. Want to go back outside now?" Tony motioned for us to leave the table. "Luanne, get on the scuba gear again." He didn't look my way. If he had, he would have seen a smug grin.

"Who's going to tell the boys at Palmetto?" I knew the answer, but I wanted him to say it out loud.

"I'll go with you after I secure this place. Mr. Pasquin, you need to stay here—out of the way, of course. Crime scene people may need to ask you some questions."

In my car, Tony ignored my gloating. I ran over every bump I could find. "Where have the divers been so far?"

"Easy caves. The ones we've got good maps of, where most of the big mastodon bones were found. They're scared of the other caves. That's why I want you down there. Act as a guide and safety patrol. By the way, could the body have broken loose and floated into the river, maybe been taken by a gator?"

"Not likely. It could have broken loose. The current is strong in that area, but it probably would have drifted into another cave or a niche somewhere. Gators don't go down there. I doubt it could have gotten back up into the river shallows without some live human help."

"Either she's still down there somewhere, or she's been lifted out—or she's gator meat."

"You put it poetically," I said.

As I pulled up in front of my house, the morning rain stopped, leaving steamy rays of sunshine.

"Get your gear and let's go," Tony said.

The cool water was going to feel good.

When we arrived on the dock, the sheriff's divers sat on the gently rocking structure. They drank sodas and bottled water, a replenishing break. The area still remained closed with yellow tape and signs indicating no swimming or tours until further notice.

People in the hotel sat on lawn chairs and rockers inside the glassed-in porch where there was air-conditioning and watched the police action. One man held a cam-corder and filmed the proceedings from a distance. A small town's version of papparazzi. It would be on the local news tonight.

I put on my gear and made a lone dive to scout the currents in the directions of the rarely explored caves. In the farthest cave, the one with an opening large enough for only one diver, I found her. Near the entrance, shoved on a shelf-like niche and held there with a rope wrapped around her neck—a woman not far into her twenties. I saw the foot and leg first, bobbing in the current in the darkened entry, the rest of her body in shadows; only the bravest of divers would ever find her. Interred deep into the spring, far removed, not even an ancient bull alligator dared look for her here.

CHAPTER SIX

Tony squinted against the hot sun. With hands on his hips, he looked down at me. "Since I loaned you that cell phone, you're a temporary agent of the law." When I didn't respond except to hand him a flipper, he added. "Now let's try and find who the hell is putting bodies in the spring."

I nodded and turned round so he would have to help me with the scuba tank. "Okay, but we need air refills down here now. Too much trouble to take the tanks into Tallahassee. Can you arrange that?" He held the tank until I had the straps firmly in place, then walked away.

Two of the divers followed me in the water, while two more followed them with a basket stretcher. The fifth diver strapped an underwater microphone onto his gear and took up the rear position in our line. We disappeared into the depths of the spring, the cold water pressing against our wet suits.

I found the cave without losing my bearings, then motioned that I would go in first. It was a tight squeeze to swim around the lady's leg and get me and my tank through the narrow opening. Once inside, the cave opened up into a grand cavern, visible only with strong lights. Two giant catfish scavenged the bottom, completely undisturbed by the humans invading their territory. They knew we could only be temporary visitors. While I waited for the two divers behind me to get through, I scanned the body, inch by inch. She couldn't have been in the water for very long. No bites. Fish would eventually make her their meal if she stayed put. One diver used his underwater camera to snap shots from different angles, then took more of the walls and opening of the cave. Handing the camera to me, he and his partner pushed close to the wall and pulled on the body. It wouldn't move. They motioned for the diver with the microphone to come through and showed him how she was attached. Through his full face mask, I could see his muscles move as he spoke to a surface recording device, making an oral record that the body was tethered to a protruding section of the cave wall. Finally, one diver moved into a curled position and forced the thin, white rope from around the protrusion. The others grabbed the body before the current shoved her downward. I held the end of the rope as they pushed her through the opening to the divers with the cage. They secured her while bracing themselves against the edge of the opening, then attached the ropes around their own waists. I watched from inside the cave as they swam in the direction of the dock.

Turning to the shelf niche, I made a quick check. In the shadow end, I found a clear plastic bag, one end torn. A substance had deposited on the bottom end where it had bunched up. If I didn't remove it carefully, the water would wash away everything. I motioned for the diver with the camera to take a picture. The other one produced an evidence bag and grasped the plastic. Shining his underwater light over the shelf, he shook his head and motioned upward with his thumb.

At the edge of the dock, the coroner stooped over the body in the basket. People who had abandoned the air-conditioned hotel stood just beyond the yellow tape. One diver handed over the camera and the bag to Tony, then we all climbed out, lifting off our tanks in full view of tourists snapping photos. Up near the hotel I could see the cam-corder still going. A truck marked Palmetto Sporting and Fishing parked at the entrance to the dock with our tank refills. Tony wasted no time. He passed the camera to a uniformed deputy who high-tailed it to a patrol car.

"What killed her?" Tony said as he leaned over the coroner who now straddled the dead girl's legs in a squat.

"Hard to say. Looks like asphyxiation of some kind." The coroner, a long, thin man with a face to match, didn't look up. "Of course, it doesn't have to be strangulation."

"What else?"

"Smothering, drowning, poison—lots of things can stop the breathing."

"Any other marks?" Tony pulled on a pair of latex gloves.

"Some bruising. Probably caused before she was dumped. If she was already dead, bumping against the cave walls would scratch the skin, but probably not bruise it. Only two scrapes on the backs of her thighs. I'll have to do some tests, but I'll bet those particles in the scrapes are going to be limestone where she brushed up against the cave wall."

"She can't be all that old," I said.

"Maybe twenty-five, maybe younger. Nails polished but short and stubby. Looks like she bites them. Toe nails polished, too. Legs shaved. Appendix scar. Look at the bluing around the nipples. Could be from the cold water, but maybe not. Have to do some toxicology on her. Blond—bottle blond—hair, black pubic hair. Eyes open, mouth open." The coroner lifted the small microphone on his lapel as he spoke.

"How long has she been down there?" Tony asked.

"Don't know yet."

"Not long," I speculated.

Tony turned and faced me. Without speaking, he waited for an explanation.

"No nibbles from little fishies, sir."

He stared at me until the coroner added, "She's right. Not down there long enough to be catfish food."

"So that places her here when?"

The coroner eyed the body again, touching the skin with his gloved hand. "I'd say yesterday or during the night. Could be dead longer than that, but I'll have to run tests. Water's too cold here to give a ballpark answer."

The coroner stood up. He was nearly six-five, all lanky-limbed, and I envisioned him in a nineteenth century black hat and tails, pacing in front of a lanterned, horse-drawn hearse. "Okay, get her into town." He waved some white-coated men to the dock where they lifted the naked lady into a zipper bag, then onto an ambulance gurney, and wheeled her to the waiting coroner's wagon.

Tony paced the dock, ripping off his unused gloves. Suddenly, he turned to two waiting plainclothes detectives. "Find out if there are any missing young women in the area. If not, look for them in neighboring states and down south."

They nodded and took off toward their cars. Tony looked up at me, hesitated, then walked the few steps to where I was sitting with my gear.

"Luanne, I want you to explore down there, but not alone. Take at least one of the guys to dive with you. I need every inch looked at."

"Every inch? Not even I—hell, not even MacAllister—has seen it all. I'll look in all the places I know, okay?" It had to come to this. I knew these waters better than anyone, but it felt good to hear Tony almost admit it.

I turned to the diver sitting closest to me, a young man with stiff blond hair that had seen too much sun. Already, he had that tanned-leather look from someone who spent time under the rays and in the water. He had stuck close to the coroner when he removed his tank, listening and watching.

"I'm Luanne Fogarty. Who are you?" I stuck out my hand.

"Jack Ellison. Am I the one who gets to dive with you?" He grinned politely, and folds of crow feet formed around his mouth and in the corners of his eyes. He would look like Pasquin in a few years.

"I hope you're a good buddy down there. It can get dangerous," I said.

"I've dived here before. Maybe I don't know the springs like you do, but I know not to mess around down there. How's your tank?"

We checked the gauges, then Jack motioned for the man with Palmetto Sporting and Fishing to bring over the dollies. We would replenish the air before going down again. I watched the other divers pick up their gear and head for the police van. The older, balding, one stopped to stare at me for a moment, then smiled, nodded, and moved on. It felt like he wanted to say, "Evenin' ma'am." I was almost sorry I hadn't asked him to dive with me.

"Tony, before we go down, I'd like to ask those teenagers a few things, like where they went in and what they saw down there. Could you arrange it?"

He gave me his usual skeptical stare, then called over an officer. He ordered the man to pick up the three boys and bring them to the springs.

Tony and I sat on the wooden seats of one side of a glass bottom boat, three scared teens on the other, a view of one medium size catfish amid swaying water grass in the middle. The boat rocked gently and every once in a while, bumped the next boat.

"I need to know some things about the night you found the old lady." Trying to act like a sweet school marm, I came across as the Nazi librarian. The boys took quick glances at each other then stared down at the glass. The catfish had found some refuse on a grass stalk to vacuum up, but I didn't think they were all that interested. I looked to Tony for help.

"You fellows said you would cooperate," Tony said, "so get to it. I can always cite you for illegal diving."

Finally, one boy, maybe the youngest, lifted his frightened blue eyes to mine. His bottom lip trembled slightly, then his mouth opened, and there was no stopping him.

"We got our new gear, and we decided to check it out in the springs. We were sure we'd be okay, and we were, really. It's just that we found that body down there."

"Start where you got into the water, and go slowly," I said.

The other two boys lowered their heads to their chins, while their buddy said it all for them.

"See, we parked the truck over on the highway, in this clump of bushes. You couldn't see it from the road. Then we hauled the gear through the trees. We'd been that way before, and we knew there weren't any bad mud holes in that part of the swamp. We got to the edge of the spring, the shallow part across from the diving tower, where it drops off pretty quick. We didn't think any gators would stay around that part."

"I've seen some swim by there, even lying on the bank."

One of the boy's pals lifted his head to speak. "But we took the chance to go in there."

"Yeah," his younger companion butted back in, "we put on the suits and the tanks right there on the shore. Hid our clothes on some bushes back in the woods."

"What time of day was this?" I asked.

"Just about five in the afternoon. We were supposed to show up at Bill's house for an eight o'clock fish fry."

Bill was the third one. He raised his head slightly, nodded, then looked back at the catfish whose long whiskers were waving around the edge of the glass.

"We had this underwater light," Bill spoke to the fish. "Even if it got dark or we got down in a dark cave, we could see all right."

I nodded. It was all I could do to keep silent. If these boys had swum into a dark cave, it wouldn't have mattered if they had a light. They wouldn't find their way out by any logic. Only luck would have guided them to safety. More people than I like to think about have disappeared in these caves, gear and all.

"Well, I knew about this one cave, and I led us to it. We saw something down there, but it was only when two of us got through the opening that I saw it was a woman." The youngest boy spoke again.

"Tell me exactly what you saw." I noticed the boy's eyes widen. His body trembled.

"She was old, had white hair. She didn't have much clothes on. And—and there was something on her head, like a bag. We got out of there fast—too fast. I bumped into the wall trying to get out and got my hand caught in that thing around her neck."

"What thing?"

"Something like a dark rope, no, more like a rubber thing, like on old cars."

"Belts." Bill said as though addressing the fish.

"Yeah. Like those belts you buy in a car parts store, only old, kind of worn. It was around her neck, then around a rock in the water behind her. I guess that's what held her down."

I leaned toward Tony and asked if he had the pictures. He handed them to me from his pocket without taking his eyes off the teens. I hadn't remembered any belt around her neck, but something had to be holding her down there. I looked at each picture, but it wasn't there.

"Is this what you saw?" I handed over the closeup of the lady.

Each boy looked, and each flinched. Bill's eyes filled with water.

"It's her all right, but she wasn't quite in this position." The youngest teen looked at the full body photo. "She was sort of turned to the side, like her feet were up here, equal with her neck."

"You mean she was horizontal to your vertical?" Amado asked.

"Yeah, that. I think the water held her feet up like that. They were like waving up and down."

"There was quite a current down there. What did you do then?"

"We got out as fast as we could." Bill had decided to talk. "We ran to the truck, dragging the tanks behind us. When we realized we'd left our clothes, we had a talk. None of us wanted to go back through those woods. We figured some kook was loose, and we told the guard at the hotel, then we had to tell the sheriff." He bit his bottom lip and looked back at the glass. The fish had disappeared, leaving only blades of eel grass to wave up at him.

Tony dismissed them with a warning to call if they thought of anything else, then ordered the patrolman to take them home.

"She was in a different position when I saw her, and there was no fan belt around her neck. Somebody—if these guys are telling the truth—changed things. Something held her body in place, but I didn't see it."

Tony nodded silently.

"Suppose—I'm making this up. Just suppose the person who put her there knew the boys had reported it, and went back in to remove the body, but I came along, and he didn't have enough time."

"He?" Tony smiled down at the catfish who returned, joined by two others.

"He, she, they?"

Tony stood up. The boat swayed in rhythm with his steps. "Could be, but they sure did it quietly. I'm taking these photos to the lab in Tallahassee. Maybe they can blow them up large enough to find what's around the lady's neck."

I returned to the dock and joined the five divers who were sitting around making jokes about pulling up a drowned body from the ocean and dozens of crabs hanging onto the skin. "Never have eaten crab again after that," said a short one, his skin in a condition of perpetual sunburn.

They made welcome noises and made a place for me to sit in their circle. I sensed slight resentment—or was it envy—in the air, but they knew I was the expert, and if any of them had to dive in the caves, I would be their lifeline. No one knew it better than Jack Ellison. He sat apart from the others, squinting as if he were perpetually smiling.

"You two getting an early start?" The older diver asked this, looking directly at me.

"Have to," I replied. "Afternoon lightning can get dangerous."

"Well, here, let me help you with this stuff. You better get some rest." He stood and began to lift flippers and masks—his and mine. The other three followed. Only Jack Ellison remained sitting on the deck. He had turned away from us and stared off across the spring.

"Vernon Drake," said the older diver, holding out his hand. "People call me Drake."

"Luanne Fogarty." I shook his hand, solid, firm grip. "And I'd like to call you Vernon, since you'll call me Luanne."

He laughed. His friendliness gave me the acceptance I needed. "You're quite a legend among divers. Maybe we could get seafood sometime. I like the stuff no matter how many crabs I've found hanging off dead men."

"I'd like that. You'll be around when we dive tomorrow?"

"Probably, unless some speed boat decides to turn over in the Ochlockonee River again. Look, Luanne, be careful tomorrow. I guess Ellison is a good diver. He wouldn't have the job otherwise. It's just that he's new, and I don't know what he's like down there. His experience is in salt water, warm oceans."

I nodded my thanks, stowed my gear, and took one last look over the spring. The shadows of cypress trees moved onto the water, darkening it to vigilant eyes. The last of the cops cleaned up, and the night guards took their stations.

Only Jack Ellison stood on the dock, gazing at the water, his hands on his hips. Maybe I should have listened to Vernon; maybe Ellison was too green to swim in caves.

CHAPTER SEVEN

Pasquin rocked in evening shadows. On the front porch, a smoke ring burned on top of an overturned terra cotta planter to keep away mosquitoes. Crickets sang, stopping only for me to walk from the car to the rickety steps.

"Child, I done ate my fried chicken sitting right here in this rocker. Thought maybe you decided to stay at the hotel again tonight." He held the screen door open for me.

"We found another body." I fell into the other rocker. Pasquin passed me a greasy box.

"Saved you a piece." Cold globs of fat nested between the skin and the meat, but I was hungry. I grabbed it without thinking. It tasted as good as had I suspected. Anything with that much fat on it has to be good—hot or cold.

"What happened at the house? Did they find anything after I left?" I knew that was why Pasquin had waited for me, his old body bursting with news.

"They told me to keep quiet, but I don't suppose that means you, does it?" He paused. "You gon' tell me about that other body?"

In the dusk, we could barely see each other, but I knew his voice and his expression. His bright old eyes glowed with anticipation.

"You tell me, I'll tell you," I said.

Pasquin's cajun voice danced around a tale of finding a man's name on some gas credit slips—a Quinlan Rentell—a salesman who traveled throughout the area. Cops were on the lookout for him. But the best part was the blood drop on the chair and traces of it on the clean kitchen floor.

"Tony says it looks like maybe somebody cut a finger, dripped a spot on the chair. On first view, you wouldn't notice the floor, but if you got down on your knees and looked hard at the linoleum like this young lady in a white coat did, you could see some tiny dots. And that young lady could actually smell the stuff. Faint odor, she said. That meant it was fresh. 'Course Carmina could have cut herself, but they don't think so. Something happened in that house—mayhem or accident."

"But no marks turned up on Carmina's body," I said. "You think Delia came around?" I hesitated. "You don't think Carmina would have done anything to Delia, do you?"

Pasquin's rocker slowed to a stop. He didn't answer except to make three little disapproving grunts.

My neck ached from the tension. I leaned back in the rocker, gazing up at a clear sky, at a moon shining directly onto the water. We could see the reeds and cypress thirty yards away better than we could see each other. Tony would be back at Carmina's house right now, spending most of the night there or with the crime lab techs. "What do you suppose all this means?"

"Young lady, I been sitting here in the twilight, now in the dark, waiting for you to tell me about the other body in the spring. Don't ask me to think until I hear your story." His slow rocking resumed its rhythmic beat against the floorboards.

"Woman in her twenties, disposed of in a similar manner. I found her in the far cave. Did you know that little opening is the doorway for one giant hole in the ground? I could feel the water currents in there. Must be lots of water jets shooting out of that place, meeting somewhere in the middle. There's also some source of light. We had lamps but I could make out the white walls in the distance."

"You scare me when you talk like that, Luanne. I know you're planning on going searching in there, and without that fellow—what was his name?"

"Harry MacAllister. Yes, if I explore, it will be without him. We never really looked into that cave. It's far away from the others. Just never got around to it."

"You never got around to getting married, neither." He pronounced married almost like marred, a better way to put it, I thought.

"Nope."

"Why didn't a pretty thing like you take a husband, anyhow?"

Pasquin again practiced the old Southern custom to pry if a girl decided to become a woman without a man, to stay single and support herself. I resented it, but it was hopeless. Relatives and acquaintances alike probed, then suggested, and finally made excuses.

"Too pretty, I guess," I said and thought about the stiff strands of gray infiltrating the brunette on my head.

"Now, ain't no gal too pretty for marriage."

"I have no idea why. I aimed at a career, at doing things with my career, not at being a wife. It hasn't bothered me, you know." I could hear his straw hat moving back and forth, fanning away my ideas.

"County going to spray down here soon," he said after awhile. "Maybe then we'll get relief from these biting critters."

I closed my eyes and gently rocked the chair back and forth

on the old boards. They groaned out a rhythm while the frogs sang a chorus. I heard Pasquin rise from his chair.

"Best get on home. Hope these flashlight batteries don't give out on me."

"You're an old swamp beast. You'll find your way even in the dark."

"Yeah. Just like old rattler and young Mr. Moccasin." He let the screen door bump gently against the frame. I opened my eyes long enough to see his light shining through the trees, then gradually fade to darkness.

I don't know how long I slept in the rocker, but I know what woke me. The frog and cricket noise stopped abruptly. The swamp, silent, vigilant, told me I'd better be vigilant, too. I moved forward silently, as quickly as the rocker would let me out of its woven seat, and latched the screen door. I had tried to patch the tear the raccoons had made by poking the ends back into the door frame. It gave the semblance of repair, but another 'coon would make light of it. I tiptoed across the porch and slipped inside the house, closing the wooden door behind me. I had taken a deep breath when I heard a knock on the screen frame.

Reaching for the toilet plunger I'd left there when I scared off the 'coons, I peeked through a narrow slit between the boards, turning on the porch light at the same time. A face stood outside the screen, almost bodiless at first, eyes wide, mouth slightly open. When my eyes adjusted to the glare, I saw a large tattoo on his fat right arm that poked out from an undershirt.

"You got any spare gasoline? We ran out and can't get back to the hunt camp."

There was a hunt camp on private property about three miles down the river, a sore spot with conservationists. The state was in litigation to buy it, but so far, it remained a hunt camp. Summer is

67

not hunting season.

"Sorry, but if you'll wait, I'll call the gas station to bring some out to you. How far up the road are you?" I knew the worthless cell phone was still in the car.

He didn't answer, and I held my breath that he hadn't checked the phone lines. Any robber with any sense would know I didn't have a phone.

"Well, I guess..." He stopped when other footsteps approached.

"Come on, Zull, we flagged down this guy on the road. He's got some spare gas in his truck." A high-pitched male voice came out of the night, followed by a wiry guy, so skinny he reminded me of a jerky little puppet.

"Thanks, ma'am." He turned and faded into the dark. I moved to a window and watched two male backs, one large and cumbrous, the other thin and bobbing about, move through the trees. Turning off the light, I sighed with relief. Pasquin was right, I would have to lock these doors more often. I returned to the porch. The moon sat high in the sky where it lit the forest around the porch all the way to the river bank.

Zull? Why would anyone be called Zull? What were people doing at the hunt camp during off season? I began to suspect everyone. Two dead women, one elderly, the other young. I'm right in the middle. Maybe it's a serial killer hitting all ages. I laughed at the same time I shivered, as I listened to the forest. It was singing again—frogs, crickets, some night birds, even that bullfrog had returned and kept up a bass beat. A familiar putt-putt sounded on the river. I looked out to see the light on a small boat follow the bends toward deep water, away from my landing.

I closed and locked the wooden door, then placed the back of a dining chair under the knob, a silly act because anyone could rip open one of the old screens, knock out the living room window, and climb inside. Of course, I hoped such a racket would wake me.

I kept a gun upstairs, and I knew how to use it.

CHAPTER EIGHT

Jack Ellison stood on the dock like he'd been waiting for hours when I arrived. I had left my tank with the Palmetto Sporting truck. It sat beside the others, a temporary sticker on it read: L. Fogarty.

"You ready?" Ellison approached me, his eyes baggy and bloodshot. Either he drank or he hadn't slept well. The thought made me nervous. His yellow, sun-bleached hair stuck out in all directions, like he had applied oil but never combed it.

"Yeah," I said. "Look, we'll dive in only one cave per day. I've got a map of the area. You can take it down with your gear. Some of these caves get really deep and shoot off in all directions. Stay with me. I've got a red and black wet suit and a yellow weight belt. What's yours?"

"Dark blue sheriff's department issue. I do have a weight belt somewhere. It's red. You wearing a buoyancy?"

"I brought one, but down there, I've always felt more comfortable without it. The currents aren't bad until you get inside a cave that has several source holes. Then you can be dragged just about anywhere. Buoyancies just make it more cumbersome to stay put."

"You've been in a lot of these caves, right?" Ellison's eyes squinted and unsquinted like a blinking warning light.

"Yes, but not all. Some are tight squeezes. I've probably looked inside most of them with a light. Why?"

"Just want to be sure you know where you're going. You carry a compass?" He asked.

"Always. Knowing which direction you're swimming in can save your life, especially if you find yourself surrounded by limestone walls. Plus, I'm attaching these this time." I held up the direction lines with their triangular attachments. As I swam into a cave, I would attach the line to a wall, then place a delta chip with its pointed end turned toward the way out. "You ready now?"

He looked at me for a few silent moments, his nearly colorless blue eyes staring through suntanned crow's-feet. "Okay, let's do it."

Tony stood, fully suited, on the dock with some other detectives. They had brought a card table, but gave up trying to use it on the floating structure, and commandeered a glass bottom boat to use for on-sight headquarters.

Tony stepped down into the boat, then turned back and called to me. "Where will you start?"

"In the far cave. We'll follow this map, but unless we can do this fast, we won't dive but once a day. Too strenuous on the body."

"Once?" He frowned, and I immediately felt the blood rise to my neck.

"Look, I know you wish MacAllister were here instead of me, but even he wouldn't go down there more than once a day. It's cold and deep and damn scary—even to MacAllister. I can't risk nitrogen build-up. Take it or leave it."

He held up his hand in a sort of Indian peace sign. "Okay,

Luanne. Back off. I'm trusting you. But don't tell me not to question what I don't know."

"See this flag?" I held up the traditional red with white stripe flag on a stiff pole that sits atop a float. "We'll situate it above the cave entrance. I'll wear a full face mask with a recorder to let you know what's happening. Ellison will carry a writing slate and note anything out of the ordinary. One thing we will not do is go opposite ways. We'll stay together, in sight of each other all the time."

"Sounds fine." Tony gave in.

"Be sure you have plenty of warm drinks for us when we come up."

"Whenever you're ready." Tony relaxed his grip on the sides of the doors.

"Pasquin told me about the house search. You're looking for a Quinlan Rentell?"

"Damn! I told the old bastard to keep it shut." He smiled slightly, knowing Pasquin would keep no secrets from me. "Yeah, you ever hear of Rentell?"

"Nope, but I'm wondering if we're going to find him down here." I pointed to the springs.

In full diving regalia, Jack Ellison and I fell back into the water, our heavy equipment making the tiniest splash. We swam just below the surface to the far end of the spring, then resurfaced above the cave entrance. I set the flag buoy over the spot, waved to Amado, then went under. Ellison followed.

We adjusted our weights and swam comfortably to the depths. Reaching the entrance where we found the young woman, we took turns moving inside the narrow opening. Each of us held a light, but, so far, we didn't need it. The bottom sheered off dramatically, almost directly downward. Attaching a direction line gently to a cave wall, I gave Jack the down hand sign, and he darted off toward the sand. I wanted to reach out and grab him; he swam too fast, but it was too late. He tried correcting himself and ended up scraping his flippers along the bottom. This was just what I didn't want, something he should have known not to do. He managed to stir up sediment to a white cloud that completely obliterated my vision for several minutes.

I stayed very still, hoping the sand would settle quickly. I spoke into the microphone, recording everything that happened, expletives included. I didn't want to get angry; that could be dangerous underwater.

When the sand finally settled enough for me to see throughout the cavern, there was no sign of Jack. His dark suit and colorful belt should have stood out against this white background, but I could sight him nowhere. *It'll be a cold day in hell before I dive with you again, buddy.*

Should I go back up and report him lost or swim around and try to find him? Suddenly, a blue wetsuit emerged from what seemed like the wall itself. Jack waved for me to follow him.

When I reached him, I realized what he had done. After stirring up sediment behind him, he found an off-shoot cave, and swam inside it. Damn bastard could have drowned in there by himself! He swam back inside, and I followed, cursing into the recorder all the way. His slate hung loose. The tether from his diving bag had stretched too far. I tapped his arm and pointed to it. He quickly stuffed it inside the bag. I motioned again that he should be taking notes on it, but he shrugged and swam to a wall.

This cave off-shoot was a limestone lover's dream. Not only a grand hole itself, it was pocked with niches. Things could be stowed in them, hidden for years, but none big enough for a body.

With my light, I did a thorough search of each little hole, finding nothing. The height was less than seven feet. Ellison searched the floor, occasionally stirring up sand with his hand. I finally motioned to him to stop and follow me out. *Somebody's got to teach this guy not to cloud the water!* I hoped his supervisor heard that.

Back in the large cavern, gouged out of the limestone over the centuries, I was reminded of my insignificance. A few catfish swam near the bottom where clumped strands of eel grass grew.

Not wanting Jack to stir up more sand, I went down to look through the grass. Nothing. Then Jack came and motioned toward another wall. Here was another hole, large enough for only one person at a time. I shone my light inside. It seemed to be a tunnel of limestone, not completely dark. I shut off my light. A murky haze glowed at the far end. Again, attaching the direction line to the wall, I motioned for him to follow me.

We swam for nearly fifteen minutes, taking care not to bump the walls, for here the limestone turned soft. One scrape and we could muddy our view for precious minutes with crumbling debris. Suddenly, we found ourselves in a space open to the sky. Old tree trunks lay on one sloping side, and a gator swam above us. We were in a sinkhole!

I gave the thumbs up to surface. Slowly, we made our way to the top. I realized then that the tunnel we had been through gradually sloped upward. When we surfaced we found ourselves in the middle of a swimming hole, surrounded by preteens swinging off tree vines, hitting the deep water with Tarzan yells. All the banks were steep except one side, the side where I had seen the gator. Trees, picnic tables, and cars covered the area above the steep banks. I never knew Palmetto Springs was connected to the Hollowell Sink!

Jack and I looked at each other, shrugged, then both of us

gave the down sign to return to the spring. We retraced our movement through the tunnel, then swam around the cavern once again. We found no more caves, only small, dark holes the size of basketballs where water shot from a secret source.

We resurfaced at the flag, swam to the dock and let the sheriff's crew help us out of the wetsuits. Jack sat next to me, drinking from an Evian bottle.

I leaned over to him, my blood boiling, and said, "Don't ever do that again, you idiot!"

He didn't look at me, but stopped mid-drink, then asked, "What?"

"Stir up the sand and head off by yourself. That's how too many people have drowned down there."

Ellison stared at nothing for a moment, refusing to look at me, then smiled, and continued drinking.

Tony handed me a warm, sweet drink. "Get cleaned up. We'll talk," he said.

"He's danger, Tony. I won't dive with him again."

"I'll transfer him to another project." Tony raised his hands in mock surrender. "What about the old guy? Is he better suited to you?" He aimed for sarcasm, but I knew Ellison's antics bothered him.

"Don't get cute. You haven't the emotional stamina for it. Yeah. Get Vernon Drake. He may know better than to go off and leave his buddy in a film of silt. And, he's not that old."

"Let's talk about the springs." Tony deliberately changed the subject. "You say this large cavern had a tunnel that led to Hollowell Sink. Any park visitors see you guys out there?"

"I don't think so, but I really couldn't say for sure. We surfaced in the middle of the sink, but we didn't keep our heads out of water very long."

"How did you end up in the middle of the sink? That hole must be, what, two hundred yards in diameter."

"It seems the sink wall kind of curves rather than goes straight down. The angle we came out of the tunnel puts us in the middle if we swim to the surface." I traced a crude diagram with a wet finger on the dock surface.

"I'm going to Hollowell Sink later today. Maybe somebody started from there and swam into the cave."

"And dragged a full-size, dead-weight body through that tunnel? There's room for only one person at a time. He'd have to tie the body onto his waist and pull it through. Then he'd have to swim through the large cavern, through the opening, guide the body through the opening, swim across the spring to the cave near the boats, and secure it there. That's nearly impossible for the most experienced diver."

"True." He paused, his dark eyes looking out across the spring. "But, he needed a place to hide some bodies."

"If I had to hide a body, I'd choose the nearest secure place. Now these caves can be pretty secure, provided no teenagers decide to try out their new diving equipment. But, they'd also have to be accessible enough to make them practical."

"We're looking for someone with territorial familiarity, someone who dives and knows the caves."

I shrugged. "Your brilliance overwhelms me."

"Who knows these springs?"

"I do. Most divers in the area. Lots of swimmers. MacAllister."

"He's in Arizona."

"Sorry, sir." I frowned. "Too bad you can't arrest him."

I slept fitfully that night. Jack Ellison kept appearing at the bottom of the cave, kicking sand in my face. In spite of my protests and my mask, the sand stung my eyes. Then I heard a boat come closer. I awoke, startled, and surrounded by two nasty mosquitoes buzzing above my head. No sooner had I smashed both of them, than three others invaded my space. I stomped into the bathroom to look for the bug spray on the window sill. Then I remembered I had used it on the screen porch. I turned on the light and clomped down the stairs in my Dr. Scholl's. They would have wakened swamp zombies, wood against wood. Turning on the porch light, I peeked outside. No bug spray. I decided to try the kitchen supplies. Turning off lights behind me, I traveled the length of the hall, past the room I planned to use for a formal dining area, and finally into my put-together kitchen. Pulling the fan light, I felt the downward breeze hit my perspiration, chilling me momentarily.

Finding the spray under the sink, a temporary metal job with matching cabinets, I stood up to get a drink of water. Two more mosquitoes buzzed in a holding pattern just above the window sill. Now I knew why. The screen, carefully torn, possibly cut, on the bottom and side just where it touched the window frame, one corner slightly bent inward, admitted the pests to a mosquito convention. Had it admitted anything else?

Jittery now, every creak in this old swamp house sent waves of primeval fear up my spine. I knew I wouldn't sleep. Hell! I feared going back up to my room. I had a choice. I could take a kitchen knife and check out every room and closet in the place. I could hike off in the dark to Pasquin's. I could run to the Honda, drive away from here, and use the cell phone on the highway. Nothing seemed plausible. My gun lay upstairs in the bedroom. I would get gray hair, or snake bit, from running through the swamp at night. Not only that, the keys to the Honda were in my bag—also in my bedroom. In my rush to move back to my roots, I had backed myself into a dangerous corner at two in the morning.

Tired of shivering in vulnerability, I felt anger boil up from my gut. My first alternative won out. I would not let anyone invade my home, and if someone was here, I would give him the fight of his life. Grabbing a large butcher knife from the wooden block and a flashlight from under the sink, I planned to search the house, room by room, turning on all the lights as I went. I slipped off the Dr. Scholl's.

In the kitchen, I jerked open the free-standing metal cupboards. Filled with boxes and crockery, no person larger than Tom Thumb could hide inside. I tiptoed to the back of the kitchen where I kept a washing machine and dryer on a make-shift enclosed back porch. Nothing. I moved back into the hall and slipped into the dining room. A large room, one that could hold a hutch, a long antique table with six full size dining chairs, and a buffet, its light switch was on the other side of the room. I used the flashlight instead, moving it around the room. I almost lost my water when my reflection flashed in the mirror on the opposite wall. Emboldened, I walked directly to the switch, flipped it on, and saw nothing, at first. Then I noticed the large cloth placed over the table to protect it from dust. Anyone could be underneath that table. I readied the knife and stooped down. Lifting the cloth, I jumped when I saw the boxes. My boxes. Winter clothes, mementos, linguistic stuff. I had placed them there for temporary storage; there was no room for anything or anyone else.

I headed for the downstairs bathroom, even more ancient

than the one upstairs. A metal chain turned on the light. The bear-claw tub sat silently, unrevealing of the ghosts that had used it over the years. Back in the hall, I dreaded opening the closet where I kept raincoats and winter things—large enough for a human. I imagined Zull packed inside with his deer rifle, just waiting to smash me against the wall like some pesky mosquito. He wasn't there.

Next, the living room. I groped for the light switch. The room blazed into view and greeted me with silence. Time to try the upstairs where there were three familiar rooms, and two under heavy repair. Only boards, nails, and saws lived in those rooms. I tiptoed as softly as anyone can on old stair boards, dodging the hole at the top. In my own room first, I quietly slipped my hand into the bedside table drawer and pulled out the pistol. It was always loaded. No way would I leave the knife lying around. Instead, I placed the flashlight on the floor by the bed, then traveled through the rooms with a weapon in each hand.

No one was anywhere unless this old place had secret spaces behind the walls, and I knew better than that. I stood at the top of the stairs, wondering if I should go back down and retrieve the bug spray. Suddenly, everything went dark. There was no sound at all. I tried to tell myself this was a power outage—common in these parts. I backed into my room to grab the flashlight. Then I did what some lower life forms do when terrified. I froze. For nearly twenty minutes I stood in that dark house and listened for movement. Nothing but mosquitoes who had again found my tasty skin buzzed around me. They brought me to reality.

I turned to the window for a moment, and something caught my eye. The electricity came back on, just in time for me to see a form—I could swear they were legs in jeans—dive into the palmetto bushes.

Back in bed, I shook for hours, falling asleep around five. Just before I dozed off, I had a revelation. If a person did dive into palmettos, he would have scratched himself in lots of places. Look for scratches, I told myself as I drifted into a stillness those two mosquitoes deliciously appreciated.

CHAPTER NINE

"If you could order those construction people out here, some of this work would get done before I'm toted off by a team of serial killers," I snapped.

I paced the floor while Tony and Loman checked out the window. I'd had no sleep; diving was out for today. Waking with a start around seven-thirty, I had again tried the cell phone on the landing and down the road. It was, appropriately, in a dead spot. I tramped across a dewy swamp to use Pasquin's phone. He was in a state of sleep, his hair a tussle of white moss atop a droopy-jowled face. He wore a frayed plaid robe, and from all the knees and hair sticking out, I'd be willing to say he had on nothing underneath. Large knotty veins stood out on his gray-haired, bowed legs. He motioned me to the phone, then waved and headed back to his bed. After calling Tony, I left, hoping Pasquin would at least get up and lock his door behind me.

"We aren't in the habit of ordering private companies about," Tony grumped back at me, "but I'll see what I can do. You sure choose some quaint little outfits, don't you?"

"It's the only one willing to drag supplies out here. The road isn't the best in the world, as you may have noticed."

"Since you can't sleep, why don't you ride into Tallahassee with me and talk to the phone company? Staying out here like a hermit is mighty dangerous for someone who's found a couple of dead women. Besides, I have to talk to the state crime lab people about the latest gem we found in the spring."

He was right. I wouldn't sleep, and I did need a phone. We left the house locked up tight, the kitchen window boarded over after the cops dusted for prints. I knew the place could still be violated. All anyone had to do was push a little on the porch screen, then on the wooden door. It was warped, and the lock didn't fit snugly anymore. But, what the hell, nothing inside was worth stealing—except my laptop computer and a tiny television that picked up two stations clearly. I carried the gun with me, something else that would make good burglar fodder.

Tony's unmarked sedan bounced over deep ruts and puddles, then settled down like a psycho on Valium when it reached the paved road. When we finally reached the highway, he glanced at me with concern and said, "How in the world do you live back there?"

"It's nice. Calm most of the time, and I've got a great big house all to myself. It'll be better when I get it insulated, a heat pump put in for heat and air, and of course, some decent kitchen appliances."

"That's going to take forever. You said you took off a year. Take you six years to do all that—and pave that old road."

"I can live here when I return to teaching. The university is only fifteen miles one way." I leaned back against the worn seat. The thought of teaching again depressed me. I might be afraid some nights, but I owned myself in that swamp, my creativity—whatever that was. I relished going to bed at night to the songs of crickets and night birds, then waking in the morning to chirping in the tree branches that stretched way over the roof of my house. I loved the sound of thunder, and rain pelting the tin roof and palmetto fronds. I could see the river from upstairs, watch a water bird dive to grab hold of a snail, then sit on a cypress knee and spread its wings to dry. Sometimes I would go down to the old landing, a little pier my daddy had built some years back. The water there was clear with only a few strands of eel grass at the bottom. When things got too much for me after Daddy died, I'd sit and gaze into that water at the baby fish who took refuge in the shallows. Occasionally, noisy mallard ducks swam nearby. I once saw a fawn come to the shore to drink. Like a sentry, I kept my eye out for alligators while it drank, ready to toss a branch at the beast if it even looked like it would eat the baby. Leaving all that to return to students who had to take the required linguistics courses, who wrote papers full of mechanical errors—not now, please.

"I'll take the gators," I mumbled. I think Tony asked what I said, but I didn't answer. Instead, I slept the rest of the way to Tallahassee.

"Wake up, Sleeping Beauty, we're at the castle," Tony announced.

I looked out the car window at the large parking lot, its asphalt dotted with oak trees. We sat at the rear of a building built on two tiers, the front at street level. My legs felt like cement logs, but I crawled out the door. At the basement-level opening, Tony held the door for me as I trudged inside a barren hallway, then upstairs to his office.

Tony's office looked like a basket of tussled laundry; books, evidence boxes, files, papers, odd tools were everywhere. To offer me a seat, he had to clear the three plastic chairs in front of his metal desk. His own swivel chair hadn't escaped the storage sentence. Picking up several files, he placed them on top of others in a wire basket on his desk, the wire part nearly invisible under its weight of paper.

Someone had tossed a worn green pillow in one of the chairs. I took it, and sat down to hear the dead girl's pathology. I didn't have to wait long. In walked two men: Marshall, from the state crime lab, and Loman.

"Girl—woman," Loman took a guilty peek at me, "about twenty-three, five-six, one hundred thirty-two pounds, dark hair dyed blond, brown eyes, hirsute like Mediterranean types, non-virgin," he took another sneak peek at me, and I nodded like it was okay. "But no sexual violence indicated, strangled before she hit the water." He stopped, leaned back off his overhanging belly and breathed deeply.

Marshall, twice Loman's size, was seated in one of the plastic chairs, with his legs far apart to house his enormous belly. He took up where Loman left off. "Seems the lady got it from the back, a ligature of some kind, maybe a wire. Her neck cut in places. She tried to stop it from the looks of her own nail scratches on her neck. Probably poked herself trying to get her fingers between the ligature and her neck. And that took some doing since she'd bitten her nails to the quick. Some debris under the nails. May be from her assailant, but we're still running tests to see if it's just her own skin. No signs of recent rape, natural or otherwise..."

"Natural rape? What's that?" I stifled a laugh.

"Sorry, bad choice of words. Not with a natural rapist's tool, e.g., the penis, nor with a Coke bottle." Marshall spoke without looking at me. "There are, however, multiple bruises around the stomach area and something that looks like old burn marks on her upper arms and thighs. If I didn't know better, I'd think the lady had been battered about a little. Maybe by a boyfriend, a husband, or a father. Traces of butterscotch hard candy in her mouth and throat. Might have been sucking on one when the assailant throttled her. Between the time he killed her to the time she hit the cold water, her leftover body heat melted the candy. Body was quite cool from the water. The time of death is a bigger estimate than usual. But, I'm guessing about thirty-six to forty-eight hours." He stopped and took a deep breath.

"So she could have been dead at the same time as our missing woman?" I sat up straight, asking the question in Tony's direction.

"There does appear to be a connection, Luanne. I mean they both turned up in spring caves." Tony spoke to his desk where he rifled through the myriad papers before him. "There was something here a few hours ago... Here!" He grabbed a file that held a single paper.

"Girl's uncle reported her missing, said she never came home from work. Then her office reported she never called in. Cops found her house messy, but nothing that looks like a struggle. Angelina Stephoulous, twenty-three. Here's the photo the uncle gave us."

"That's the one." Marshall handed the five-by-eight portrait of a sexy woman who, with a little eyebrow plucking, and a makeup job with Aida Grey, may have passed for a peroxided Sophia Loren at that age.

"Anything from Washington?"

"We tried the fingerprint match, but she evidently had none on file."

"That's rare these days. Says here she worked for Angel's Bay Seafood Company. They're in the next county but have an outlet here. She was their Tallahassee branch bookkeeper."

"They catch it or can it?" Marshall asked.

"Catch it and sell it fresh. They're on the west side of town. Why?"

"Just wondered. State health found some tainted cans and pulled them from the markets. Thought maybe she could know something, and they whacked her. I guess that's an old glamorous mob story." Marshall took a deep breath that elevated his entire front for a moment, then lowered it on the exhale.

"We're going over there. You care to join us, Marshall?" Amado grinned at the heavy man whose upper thighs hid all evidence of plastic seating.

He grunted a negative, then pushed his pounds out of the straight chair. "You can...nah!"

"What?"

"Pick up two, three pounds of mullet for me?" He shoved his hands in his pocket and pulled out two five-dollar bills.

Angel's Bay Seafood Market consisted of a long, cement-block building housed between the walls of the old city cemetery and what is locally known as French Town. The area, primarily black now, was Cajun territory long ago. I imagined Pasquin's family passed this way once. Tiny wood-frame houses bordered the streets lined with grand oaks, their moss draping to the buckling sidewalk. On sagging wood porches, black women sat with toddlers who cried in their laps; older ones played about the dirt yards. The streets here are narrow, built in the days before Model T's.

My body told me to stay in the back seat and nap, but my curiosity pushed me out with the detectives. We entered the gray structure, its floors and walls little different from the outside cement. Someone had taped sales signs for this kind of fish and that kind of crab on the rough blocks. In the first large room, rows of glass-fronted ice cases stood in formation, each one holding dead-eyed fish either local or imported, fresh or salt water.

Another room led off from this one, and more ice cases displayed shellfish: oysters from Apalachicola, shrimp from the Gulf of Mexico, some all the way from Malaysia, crab from Panacea. The back door led outside to tanks of live fish, imported lobster, and crab taking their last splash before decorating a dish. Beyond the loading dock, more cold gray cement. At the very end, there was a tiny room with a heavy metal door and a small window to see outside. The sign read Office. A window air conditioner pumped cold air inside, probably to keep the boss as cold as the dead fish.

The man, a fat-armed portly, who slicked back his hair with lemon-smelling pomade, must have seen us coming. He threw open the office door just as Tony rang the bell.

"You the law, I suppose. Thanks for not wearing uniforms. All I need is the semblance of legal trouble down here. Every time some uniform shows up, punks get the idea I've been ripped off again; they think it's their turn. You want to know about Angie, right?"

"Yes, Mr. Petroulious." Tony and Loman flashed their badges for the record. "When did you see her last?"

"I told all that to the cops the other day. She left work early on Monday last. Haven't seen her since. Her father said she never got home. What can I tell you?"

Arno Petroulious wouldn't sit down. He paced the tiny office, chewing but not lighting a cigar. His stocky build was too heavy for his short frame, and in the fish-blood-smeared whites he wore, he looked like a wadded-up dirty handkerchief. I guessed the pomade was to overpower the fish odor. It barely disguised it.

"What time did she leave work?" Loman asked.

"Around four-thirty. No need for a bookkeeper to stay long hours unless it's tax time."

"And she went straight home or at least in her usual direction?" Tony scanned the tiny office.

"Beats me. She parks out back here alongside the rest of us. Her car was gone. I don't watch how she drives off."

"If she had gone in the direction of home, she would have gone south, right?" I said.

"Can't. This is a one-way street. She'd have to go north one block and turn one way or the other. I don't know which way that was."

"Turning west would take her towards the cemetery, east toward the capitol, right?" I drew a map in my head.

"Yep." Petroulious pounded out the unlit cigar in an ashtray. He had the nervous habits of a man trying to break the smoking habit. I wondered if his health was bad; his size, the cigar, his hyperactivity, all the makings of a bad heart.

"Was she friendly with any of the employees, sir?" Loman asked. His half-open eyes had examined the room, too. He nodded slightly to Tony. It would take a team a week to find anything in this place. It was packed as tightly as its owner.

"Got along with everybody, but I didn't see any, well, hanky-panky, if you know what I mean."

"We need to question everyone. Can you make sure no one leaves, and give us a place to work?" Tony stood.

"Stay here. I'll get the guys."

Loman followed him out. I took a metal chair in a corner while Tony took Petroulious' desk chair. That left one seat for whoever would be questioned. Petroulious returned with a scraggly-haired young man in jeans and fish-bloodied tee shirt.

"Mr. Petroulious, did Angie know anything about scuba diving?" I asked.

"Her? Not hardly. She didn't like the sun at all, made her

dark, she said." Mr. Petroulious squeezed around the desk, frowning at Tony who occupied his seat. The young man stood in the open doorway letting the cold air blow outside.

"Does anyone in the company scuba dive?" I continued.

"We got one guy who does. Goes out for fun, and sometimes helps the boats out when we can't find another diver down at the coast. You want to talk to him?" Petroulious stuck the flat-ended cigar back into his mouth.

"Can you get him?"

As soon as he went off to find the employee, I told Loman to be on hand for the questioning. Tony had an expressionless spasm, but I didn't care. I was the diving expert.

I left the closet-sized office and stood on the cement loading dock. Someone had used a hose to wash away old blood and scales, and water puddled in places where the cement had worn down. Loman followed me and leaned against the wall.

A tall man in a leather apron approached us. His thinning blond hair sat atop skin that had taken on the hue of his scaly merchandise. "I'm Frank Ellison, ma'am. You wanted to see me?"

Loman identified himself, then introduced me as a diver with the sheriff's office.

"Do you ever dive in the springs around the Palmetto River?" I asked.

"Not much. I have for fun, with friends. It's not a place I get around too often. Mostly, I dive in the Gulf. Prefer the warm water."

"Did you know Angelina Stephoulous?" Loman's voice sounded behind me.

"Yeah. She was the bookkeeper here. I was damn upset by her disappearance."

"Did she ever dive with you?" I continued.

"Never. In fact, I never did anything with her. When she first got here, I wanted to ask her out, but she made it clear that her daddy was Greek, from the old country. She didn't date— ever. Can you imagine? In her twenties and still following orders from Daddy." The man's small eyes darted around, never connecting with mine. He ran his hand through the thin hair.

"She never socialized with anyone here?" Loman asked.

"I think she may have had lunch with the two ladies who shuck oysters, but I wouldn't call it socializing. They were just women who could keep her away from the company of men."

"How did she get along with the boss?" Loman stood beside me now.

"Her uncle? At least that's what she called him. I don't think they're related, just Greek. That's why her old man let her work here. Had a countryman on hand to look after her virginity." He stared at me suddenly. The squinting crow's-feet around his pale blue eyes looked familiar.

I thanked him, then watched him go back to checking in crates and sending them off to various cold spots. Something about his tale didn't ring true. He couldn't tell it without fidgeting and looking down at his feet. I suspected that even if he hadn't dated Angie, he had at least felt her up in a storage room a few times. As I turned back into the office, he called after me.

"Ma'am! I've got a brother that works with you guys. You probably know him—Jack Ellison."

CHAPTER TEN

I huddled against the patrol car door, my eyes burning from lack of sleep. Loman headed across town to the phone company.

Tony spoke from the passenger side of the patrol car. "You going to be rested enough to dive tomorrow?"

"Yeah, but only if you get Vernon Drake. No more Jack Ellison. I wonder if his brother is as careless as he is."

"I've never known Jack to be careless before."

There it was, that comment with a hint of mistrust, a challenge to female competence.

"I'm not getting into it with you, Tony. I'm just too tired. Get Vernon or do without me." I closed my eyes, waiting for the next snide remark, but there was silence until Loman spoke.

"One of the items found in Carmina Twiggins' house was a tin of butterscotch candies. Found cellophane in a trash can near the table. We figure she had just opened them. Maybe we can find out where she bought them."

"Or," I interjected with my eyes still closed, "who brought them to her as a gift. And, why did Angie Stephoulous have one of them in her mouth—if it came from the same tin? Maybe she was visiting the old lady, along with Delia."

"What makes you think they were a gift?" Tony asked.

"I'd never buy expensive candy for myself. Butterscotch in a tin sounds costly. It's the kind of thing one would get for a house gift."

Before either of them could answer me, a call came for Tony. His people had located Carmina's boarder, Quinlan Rentell.

"Look, we've got to get to Tifton right now," he said. "I can drop you off at the phone company and have a deputy drive you home, or," he hesitated, "you can come with us."

I settled my head on the car window, propped my feet on the seat, and said, "Take your time. I need the rest." I slept soundly all the way to Tifton, waking once when sunlight between overhanging tree branches flashed in my face, like psychedelic lights. Just before we arrived, I stretched, my neck aching, and pulled myself upright. In spite of the cramped position, I felt better.

"By the way," I said. "Who was that scraggly fellow hanging around Petroulious' market?"

"Worker at the fish house, part-time fellow, he said. Why?" Tony turned to look at me.

"Just the way he twitched about, kind of nervous, like..." I couldn't think where I'd seen those movements before. "Like somebody on something."

"Could be," said Loman. "Most kids his age got something down their gullet, up the nostrils, or in the veins. Here we are." He slowed, then stopped at a signal light.

Tifton, Georgia, an agricultural town, and a stopover for people traveling the interstate, houses fast food places next door to pecan warehouses, motels next to feed supply houses, and liquor stores next to grandma kitchens.

Loman pulled into the parking lot of Herman's Farm Store, a cement and tin place with long folding doors and a high dock for truck deliveries. In late afternoon, only one truck backed against the loading area. Tony rolled down his window and spoke to a toothless man with the Herman's logo on his sleeve. He moved his jaws up and down as though scratching his gums.

"Sheriff's Detective Amado, here to see Mr. Quinlan Rentell. Is he inside?"

"Most likely gone by now." He spat a brown dart of snuff on the gravel drive.

"He was told to wait here for me."

"Then he's in the office with the boss. Push that button by the sliding door."

The three of us climbed onto the raised dock, Loman grunting as he followed Tony and me. A girl with two nose rings answered the buzz and, between chews on her wad of gum, told us to follow her to the office. The smell of dried oats filled the air, threatening sneezes if you breathed too hard. We came to a dingy glass cubicle in a corner free of feed bags. Inside, two men chatted over beer cans.

"You Herman?" asked Tony.

"His descendant. I guess you're Amado from Tallahassee?"

The other man, thin enough to have eaten the oats he sold and nothing else, sat up straight and placed his beer can on the desk. He extended a hand to Tony.

"I'm Rentell. Local sheriff said I should wait for you here. I couldn't imagine what the trouble was."

"You do know your landlady, Miz Twiggins, is dead, Mr. Rentell?"

"No! That sweet old thing. What happened? I mean if she had a heart attack, you guys wouldn't be calling on me, right?"

"She did have a heart attack, but we need some other questions answered. Is there a place we can talk privately?"

Herman's descendant volunteered to leave the room. The rest of us sat on folding metal chairs and discussed Quinlan's routine. Rentell told us he traveled a lot, selling additives to stock feed. He had rented rooms in three different states and stayed in the closest one each night. He planned on returning to the one in Savannah tonight since he had an appointment there tomorrow.

"Were you in Tallahassee last Monday or Tuesday?"

"No. I have been in Charlotte most of the past two weeks, or places just outside there."

He gave the places and witnesses' names to Loman. Tony told him to notify the sheriff's department when he returned to Tallahassee. The man, grabbing a packet of cigarettes from his shirt pocket, stood up and reluctantly shook Tony's hand.

I bit my tongue and said, "You move like a swimmer. Do you ever scuba dive?"

His face turned from sour to questioning to a broad smile. "I did once. Bunch of us did back in our high school days. Why do you ask?"

"Ever dive in Palmetto Springs?" I looked over the scrawny body. He seemed one long bone from head to foot.

"Never. I don't trust those caves, and it's too cold. Now some of the lakes around here are fine, but mostly I dived the ocean."

"Ever meet an Angelina Stephoulous?" Tony asked the question as though he were saying grace, head bowed, no expression. Rentell's upper body stiffened, and his eyes widened.

"I don't recall a woman by that name."

"Ever deal with people who have Greek names?" I asked.

Rentell shook his head and shrugged, his bulging eyes beginning to water. If his alibis checked out, he was home free.

Driving toward Florida, I dumped all my doubts about Rentell

94

onto Tony. "The man knows there are caves in Palmetto Spring, but look at his body, for heaven's sake! He's eaten up with tobacco and alcohol. I doubt he could swim three yards. Ocean diving. Ha! No self-respecting shark would look twice at those bones."

Tony smiled at Loman. "Did look a little puny."

At seven, we pulled into the little town of Fogarty Spring. Tony decided we'd better find something to eat. I suggested the only place there was—Mama's Table.

Mama, the most recent one, was thirty-two years old. A natural towhead blond, Mama carried her Rubenesque proportions grandly through the narrow aisles of 1950's green tables and plastic booth seats. Once in a while, blue-and-white checked tablecloths appeared, but mostly customers ate from bare formica tops. Food was the ambiance here—Southern sustenance—black-eyed peas and rice, pork ribs, fatback and greens, fried shrimp, and all the mullet you can eat every night of the week. Mama's Table kept Fogarty Spring on the map. People came from miles, even from Alabama and Georgia, to sup on the generous portions and do the give-and-take tease with Mama. Part of the building that housed the eatery stood on water stilts, next to the dock. If you couldn't find Pasquin at his house, you'd probably find him fanning himself at one of these tables. The current Mama took good care of him, loving the sound of his Cajun cadence.

"I'm getting the works," Loman announced before he saw the menu. "Order for me while I use the john."

"That boy always got to use the facilities when he comes in here," Mama said as she gathered the menus. "Done got a gut so big he could use it to float down the river." She spoke loud enough for Loman to hear her as he disappeared behind the dingy men's room door. "How come the sheriff let him get so big, huh?" She didn't wait for an answer, but ran one hand down a bulging hip

95

and across a heavy thigh. "Now, he ought to stay slim as me." She laughed at her own joke and headed for the kitchen.

"Sorry about the phone, Luanne," Tony said when we were alone. "We just didn't get around to doing what we started, did we?"

"Happens all the time, Tony. Starting and not completing things is the story of my life."

"You really plan to finish that old house? I'm surprised you don't have a ton of termites."

"I did. I had the exterminators out there last month. Still, the place has to be shored up, boards replaced. It's a long project, but it gives me solace."

"I suppose sitting on that porch at twilight is restful. Better than on a cement balcony in a town apartment." Tony, in an unusual moment of reverie, droned on about the solace we need. His words became a buzz in my head.

I watched the dock. A thin man with slightly bowed legs untangled a rope. It had begun to rain, and he pulled a hood over his head. Unable to master the tangled rope, he gave it an angry jerk, which sent him stumbling to the edge of the dock. Another man came to help. Without a nod, the first one darted into the boat and full throttled up the river. In spite of the glass window pane and the indoor air-conditioning, I could hear the faint putt-putt of his motor.

"You know, Tony, I could swear I've seen that man before, and I've heard that motor."

"All motors sound alike...," said Tony, then caught himself. "Okay, sorry. Where did you hear it?"

I scowled at him, and for a moment considered silent punishment. I wondered if marriage was like this. Some of my friends said it was. "Twice, standing on my porch at night. It traveled away from me, back this way."

"Pasquin has a boat, right?"

"He's got a new motor that sounds young and healthy. That one sounds like it's been repaired once too often."

"Well, Luanne, find out who owns it, when you're not nailing on new boards."

Mama appeared and did her small talk peppered with laughter. We ordered the Southern Platter which, as Loman said, was the works—fried in cornmeal everything—then sipped iced tea while we waited. A silence set in between Amado and me. Finally, I told him I'd be right back and went out to the dock.

The light rain felt good on my face. I approached the old man who introduced himself as the dock keeper, and asked him about the small boat.

"Oh, that. Several fellows keep it down here and take turns using it. It's got an old motor that breaks down every now and then, but mostly it keeps going. To tell you the truth, I don't know who exactly owns it but I suspect it's Angel's Bay Seafood. Got it here for tax write-offs. Anyhow, most of the fellows who use it are employees of theirs."

Back at the table, Tony explained like an impatient father. "It's not unusual for a seafood company to keep boats on rivers. What's your point?"

"Why in heaven's name won't you indulge me at least once in a while? Why do you immediately become the adversary?"

His face reddened, and his jaw tightened. "Listen, I have to play the devil's advocate. In any police matter, I have to see all sides. Doing that makes people come out with all they know, even things they don't know they know!"

Loman buttered a wedge of iron-skillet cornbread. "Does seem odd we've run into that company twice in one day. They got

97

a boat here, they got an employee's dead body there, they...." He stopped when he shoved the bread into his mouth.

Tony glared at him. We ate in silence, only once bringing up the taste of the food and how it changed from visit to visit. Mama returned to the table several times to refill the tea glasses and make a few jokes. When we didn't laugh, she said, "You folks tenser than a barracuda on a gator tail."

"Are you sure you want to go back to that house tonight?" Tony asked as we moved from the air-conditioned cafe to the muggy outdoors. "You could always get a room at the hotel until the phone company puts in lines."

"Know any way to hurry them up? They don't have a whole lot of interest in extending the service down from Pasquin's house."

Tony shook his head and made a grunting noise.

"Right. Well, I'm ready for anything tonight. The gun stays by the bed, and I'll leave lights on no matter how many bug conventions gather 'round them."

"Weather man says it may rain tomorrow morning. Is that going to stop you diving?" asked Tony.

"Depends. If it's just rain, it will silt up the shallows but not the depths. If it's lightning, we stay home."

We made arrangements to meet on the Palmetto Springs dock at eight in the morning with equipment ready to go. Loman and Tony did a quick search of the house before leaving me to the swamp creatures. As their taillights faded into the oaks, I heard the putt-putt again, the same boat returning down river.

Grabbing a light and an old hoe handle, I headed for the broken-down landing. It could be treacherous at night; the boards

98

were in worse shape than inside the house. Support poles still stuck out of the water, but the slats were rotting in places, their rusty nails poking up like little snake heads. I stepped on the places I knew were strong. At the end of the landing, small rippling wakes from the boat slapped against the posts. Unable to see the boat, I shined the light around me, then across the narrow inlet that led out to the river. This inlet was tricky. It looked like shallows next to the bank, but the bottom dropped off quickly into a deep hole as cold and clear as the deep spring on the other side. In one spot, you could feel the icy water pushing from the limestone into the cavity. Another good place to hide a body, I thought. In the morning, I would have to convince Tony to let me dive here before diving in Palmetto Springs.

The crickets and frogs stopped their chorus as I tramped through their territory, then started up again as I left it. At the foot of my front steps, I halted. Following him with my light, I watched the rusty pipe moccasin slither beneath the porch.

CHAPTER ELEVEN

Clouds covered the sky and reached down so low they formed a muggy blanket over the top of Palmetto Springs. It would rain early today. Tony wouldn't hear of diving at my landing before his official police work. "Besides," he said, "how could I justify to all these men they had to wait around half a day for you to satisfy a whim?"

That did it! "Whim?" I started to argue, but he walked away from me, heading for the refill truck that had pulled inside the yellow tape.

"You ready to go today?" Vernon Drake gripped my shoulder with a strong hand. He gave it a little squeeze before he let go.

I sat with Vernon, his long brown legs touching my bare ones. We went over the underwater route. First, the small cave next to the one Ellison and I had explored, then some smaller pseudo-caves near the main cave where I had seen the old woman's body. If we had time and energy left, we would again take a brief look around the first cave and the one where we found Angie Stephoulous.

Two more detectives and a uniformed deputy joined us on the dock. They spoke with Tony while Vernon and I donned wetsuits and tanks. Again, a small group of curious people watched from the hotel porch in the distance. Employees, more than likely.

The tourist area had been closed since the day we discovered the first body.

Vernon wore the full face mask with the communication device inside. He would voice what we found, his message recorded back on the dock. Tumbling backwards, we headed into clean, frigid water. It took only seconds to feel the rush of some primitive water faucet left running for centuries.

I headed to the first small cave, on the other side of the spring and near some thick water grass. It was not as deep as in other places. I didn't care to swim here. If a gator or snake ever decided to come into lower depths, he would do it in a grassy area like this. As we swam closer to the cave opening, I kept an eye open for dangerous critters. A few fish scoured the sandy bottom in between blades of grass. Just above the eel grass line, fuzzy aquarium grass, an ecological hazard to the area, flourished. It came from South America for tropical fish aquariums. Someone had dumped it into the springs where it took over like a swarm of locusts. If it killed the eel grass, the snails would no longer live here. No snails equaled no birds who ate snails. Thus, the cycle would be disrupted, and who knows what would happen to the area. Teams of ecologists from the university often came here to test the growth of the grass, hoping to find something in their laboratories to stop it.

I found the opening, large enough for me and my tank, swam through and motioned for Vernon to follow. We were on the opposite side of the spring from the large cave I had explored with Jack. No light source existed here; we entered pitch darkness. Turning on our lamps, we faced a large group of catfish; it was like walking into a flock of birds. As soon as the lights came on, they scurried toward the darkness. I motioned an "I wonder about this" to Vernon. Why so many catfish, a scavenger fish, in this one place? A food source here? Goose bumps rose on my neck.

Carefully, and always keeping each other in sight, we shone our lights on every inch of the cave walls and floor. The fish congregated near a back wall, on a slope in the floor of the cave. I headed for the area and adjusted my buoyancy in order to sift through the sand with my fingers. One brush with the tips and something tumbled down the slope. Just before it threatened to fall into darkness, it balanced on a ledge. Vernon swam to the ledge with an evidence net. He held it steady and brushed the sand slightly. Bones dropped, hitting the cords of the net and sending up sandy dust.

I pulled out my own net and went back to sifting the sand on the slope. Within the grains, I found the smooth top of something round, a skull. We soon had more bones—human ones—than our evidence bags could carry.

"They're human and there's more," I said to Tony as I held onto the edge of the dock, the rest of my body still in the water. Vernon handed over the bags to the detectives. A patrolman called the coroner on his car radio.

"We need more bags, and we'll have to go back," I said. "I don't know if we'll make the main cave today." Tony passed over two bottles of orange soda for us to drink before we dove again.

Two more trips into the underwater grave, and we had most of a body, maybe not all the same body. We saw no trace of flesh; catfish must have stripped it clean. If we were lucky, there would be something left to test for DNA.

Vernon helped me with my equipment. "At least the teeth are intact. The coroner may be able to make a match from them."

Exhaustion set in. We grappled with masks, flippers, and cylinders on the dock. Breathing from a tank dehydrates the body. We needed warmth and liquid, not to mention food, as soon as possible.

"You game for seafood tonight?" Vernon asked as he stripped to his bathing suit. His firm body sported gray and black chest hair that formed a narrow line between his pecs then ran to his navel where it disappeared under the yellow suit material, then reappeared on his muscular legs. His head was bald on top, the same gray-black hair forming around the sides. But he wore his baldness well, somehow enhancing his very maleness. I looked at his dark, tanned, rugged face. Bright blue eyes shone from beneath black brows, and his smile was wide. I liked what I saw.

"Got a place in mind?"

"Ever been to the Greek Oyster near St. Marks?"

"Never, but I'm game."

We made arrangements for him to pick me up at seven, giving us time for the needed rest after a dive. There would be no more diving today, anyway. Thunder rumbled in the distance, and the clouds turned black.

Vernon surrounded me with a large towel. We rested on the dock and listened to the coroner make a first sight investigation of the bones in the bag.

"I need tests and laboratory re-assortment of these, but I'll bet they're female and only from one female's body." He spoke to the bones, poking them with his gloved fingers. "Must have been dead for some time since the flesh is all gone. You say the fish were still swarming around down there? Probably cleaning off the last tidbits. And no sign of clothes? Could have been in the

103

nude when she entered the water or washed away, even disintegrated if she's been here long enough. Got to be four to five months, maybe longer, she's been down there." He stood up. "I'll let you know as soon as I know."

I reminded Tony of my landing. "It's another deep cave. Could be something there, and that boat..."

He raised his hand to stop me. "Tomorrow, okay?"

I tried to nap, but I kept telling myself not to feel like a giddy teenager with a new beau. *You thought Harry MacAllister would be the one. He didn't pan out.* Deep down bitterness stirred up its ugly acid. Vernon was an attractive diver, too.

Dressing up seemed foreign to me. I hadn't pulled on the green spaghetti-strap number since the linguistic department party last summer. Shoes with tiny buckles and high heels never fit like flippers, but I felt just as awkward walking in them. I turned my ankle when I backed up to see myself in the mirror. My short hair did its humidity kink around my face. In a back light, it made a ghostly aura around my head. A little powder covered the shiny tan face, and I dabbed on some pink lip gloss. It would have to do. It's just a dinner, an evening for two equals to enjoy each other.

When Vernon stepped onto the porch, he said, "I didn't know people still lived in places like this." He was dressed casually in a short-sleeved white shirt and slacks. "Fantastic! How did you ever find it?" He wandered every inch of the porch.

"Born to the manor, I guess." I gave him a brief tour to show him work in progress. When he expressed genuine interest in the kinds of lumber I chose, the paint, the swamp deterioration, I squelched the thought that he might be a good man to

104

have around the house.

It took us twenty minutes to reach the little town of St. Marks with its few shops and lots of docking facilities, then ten more to go down a coast road to the Greek Oyster. We parked in front of a converted house set back in the pines that lined this part of the St. Marks River, a river that eventually led into the Palmetto River. Inside, we sat at a table in a room with hardwood floors, high ceilings, and elongated windows draped with the blue-white design of Greek motif.

The waiters came right off the Greek ships. An assortment of old men, they dressed in black slacks, striped tee shirts, and deck shoes. They spoke in accents. Vernon said they were retired sailors from down around Tarpon Springs, an old Greek sponging area from years ago. Bouzukia music played over a speaker system, and, once in a while, a lusty-eyed man in an apron appeared, danced some Zorba steps, then disappeared into the kitchen.

"How come I never heard about this place?" I asked, after we had ordered the platter.

"It's not publicized. I think it's really a front for something else. Cops talk about it sometimes, even stake it out on occasion. I bet two or three eating here right now are cops."

"You're talking about drugs?"

"Never found any evidence of dealing. More like passing along information. A kind of relay point in the trade—maybe. This is all speculation, of course. I'm not in narcotics; I don't really know. By the way, old Arno Petroulious owns this place."

"Vernon, we're not going to get into any kind of trouble being here, are we?"

He laughed. "Not hardly. I've been down here with the sheriff himself a couple of times." He leaned toward me. "Luanne, relax and enjoy. I want this evening to be special."

I felt the blush against my ears. When the salads appeared, I silently thanked the River God.

Wooden bowls of lettuce, peppers, sour olives, anchovies, and feta cheese sat in front of us. Later, we consumed a platter of assorted seafood, Greek bread, baklava, and two glasses of wine for me. Vernon drank water. Vernon held my hand when we left. On our way out the door, we met another party coming in—four men, two familiar faces.

"Evening, Jack." I heard Vernon address one, then realized it was Jack Ellison, my ex-diving partner, and his brother, Frank, from Angel's Bay Seafood. Tony must have informed Jack of my refusal to dive with him again, but I didn't want that to sour the evening. I pretended to look at a large aquarium in the entry, but I couldn't avoid looking Ellison in the face as we left. He nodded without smiling; I nodded in return.

The hum of the car sang love songs to me all the way home. Vernon didn't talk much, but he occasionally reached over to squeeze my hand. He parked in the darkness beside the house.

"Be careful at the steps. I have a poisonous friend who hangs out under my porch. He's not always a safe distance away." I pointed toward the ground, lit up by the strong porch light. "I've got wine, even coffee, if you're game."

Vernon followed me up the stairs, looking on both sides for my snake. He declined wine as he had done all evening. We sipped iced tea instead in a semi-dark living room, seated close on the sofa. The windows stood wide open for precious little swamp breeze.

"You dive beautifully, Luanne." Vernon's voice was low, almost seductive in his compliment. I had a feeling diving was not on his mind. It certainly wasn't on mine. "Tell me about this snake."

He changed the subject and relaxed away from me. I wanted him near again.

"What can I say? He likes the cool, moist area under the house. Probably finds rats to eat. But, maybe he likes me. I don't try to kill him. I let him do his stuff, go his own way. He always comes back. Faithful little thing, isn't he?"

Vernon took my lightness as a signal to cuddle. He slipped his arm around my shoulder, then tousled my hair slightly with his other hand. "And deadly! Just like a man, right?" He smiled that toothy, boyish way I had seen at the dock. Even in the shadows, I could see the mischievous gleam in his blue eyes.

"Vernon?" I whispered. "Is there a Mrs. Drake?"

"Was. Two of them, in fact. None now." He stopped tousling my hair and gripped it firmly without pulling, then leaned over me. I closed my eyes and felt his lips.

Our lovemaking went like our diving—teamwork toward one goal. And we reached that goal twice in one muggy evening in the middle of a north Florida swamp. Where he led, I followed, and where I guided, he complied. Our strong swimming muscles undulated without the aid of buoyancy or currents. Finally, in the darkness, we lay as two spent swimmers on my bed, listening to crickets sing their hallelujah chorus outside. Our bodies drenched in sweat, we held hands until we drifted into deep, soothing sleep.

The dream ended close to morning when the motor passed in the distance. The dock again, I whispered.

CHAPTER TWELVE

The damp cool, by Florida standards, of the night gave way to the muggy heat of the morning; mist rose off the still inlets of the river like steam from a giant city grate. Vernon had to leave at seven to report to the sheriff's office in Tallahassee by eight. We had drifted through a quiet breakfast of cereal, milk, and fruit. We said very little out loud. I loved his tender gestures, touching my cheek, kissing my neck, holding me briefly in his arms. I loved his quiet.

As he went down the steps, he checked under the porch for the snake before laughing off to his car. Waving as he turned around on the swamp floor, he headed away from me. His car disappeared into the trees. Then I turned my attention to the misty river and wondered if Pasquin would take me out in his boat.

Risking safety, I knocked on Pasquin's door before nine in the morning. His early life of night parties on the river had formed his habit of staying up late, "communing with the dark," he called it, then sleeping until the humidity made him uncomfortable enough to want to be away from sheets. He appeared at the door, hair disheveled.

"What the hell you want now?" His grumpiness was real,

though I knew it wasn't personal. He wore the same short robe.

"Can I come in and ask a favor?"

"This early?"

"Dawn rose hours ago, and it's time you did, too. I want you to take me somewhere in your boat."

"Well, I ain't taking nobody nowhere in nothing 'til I get some café in me. Come in and wait."

Inside the dark living room, I fidgeted long enough for him to get his brew together. He hadn't turned on a single light. I walked to one of the heavy green curtains and pulled it back on its heavy brass rod. Dust particles glistened like a million little diamond dots in the intense sunlight that burst through the window. The glass panes needed washing from inside; frequent rains took care of the outside.

In the dim light, I made out miniature brass pots, carved marble dragons, and iron-studded cannons with rusted Civil War soldiers in perpetual firing stance on scarred oak end tables, interesting items that must have been antiques. From the kitchen, I heard pans clatter against each other. On one table, I found an assortment of tin boxes. They had intricate designs on the lids, faded now from lack of polishing. Each one sounded empty when I shook it. On a table beside an overstuffed chair, I found another box; its shiny exterior indicated frequent touch. When I picked it up, it felt heavy and something rattled. Inside, I faced a pile of silver dollars, some dark with age, others bright as if recently polished.

"That's a family heirloom you got there," said Pasquin as he placed a tray with two coffee cups on a table near the kitchen door. "Family's been collecting these since 'fore I was born."

"How many are in here?" I asked, embarrassed that he caught me snooping.

"Thirty, last count. 'Course that's not all I got. Rest are in a safety deposit box up in Tallahassee. I keep these around in case I run short of cash. Sometimes, like last night, I get them out and try to remember which relative left them to me and which ones I got myself." He poured dark coffee into a tea cup and passed it to me.

"Do all your relatives collect them?" I looked into the cup. The contents could have passed for mud.

"Sure do, then pass them down after they die. I think it has something to do with Cajuns being run out of town after town. Maybe saving silver dollars gave them a feeling they might not go hungry on the run. Anyhow, all us kids got them sooner or later." He sat in the heavy chair and took a loud sip from his own cup.

"Including Carmina?" I touched the hot liquid to my lips.

"All the kids."

"Then where are hers? I mean, did they find them in her house, or maybe she kept them in a deposit box, too?" I swallowed a bitter, grainy sip of coffee.

"Now that's a curious thing, ain't it? I don't remember anybody finding any in her house, and there's been no mention of a deposit box in the inheritance. I better do some checking around about that."

I took a full gulp of the strong, thick liquid that reflected Pasquin's French heritage and nearly blew off the top of my Anglo head. "How do you drink this stuff?" I placed the cup on the table.

"It gets my heart beating, girl. You want me to boat you down the river, then you let me drink my medicine." He sipped with sound effects again. "You not 'sposed to drink it like beer. You want some eggs?"

I sat at the kitchen table while Pasquin fried eggs and bacon, then warmed thick rolls. The smell of fresh cooking mixed with old odors until my head swam. I reached behind me and shoved up a window. "You need air in here, old man."

"Conditioner is on. You gon' let all the cool out."

"And the food odors."

He didn't say anymore, but joined me at the table. He changed the strong brew for a mixture of coffee with lots of cream in a soup bowl. Dipping a roll into the mixture, he ate it along with one of the heaviest breakfasts I've seen in years.

"You blow all the theories about heavy meals shortening one's life." I copied his dipping routine and found it tasty.

I watched Pasquin's wrinkled hands calmly feed himself without the shaking or slow movements of the elderly. He seemed old as the river and just as timeless.

"Okay, let me wash up a little, then we'll see about taking the boat on the river. Maybe you ought to call up Tony about those coins while I'm freshening my face." He pointed to the phone and rambled off down the hall.

I stood in the dusty window light again and phoned Tony.

"According to the list I have in front of me, the search came up with no silver dollars," he said. "I'll check the banks again, but my bet is whoever was in that house took off with them—unless the old lady spent the things. Looks like I'm going to have to put somebody on her financial state, too. Thanks for the extra work. Anything else you'd like me to do?" Tony breathed an impatient sigh.

"Yeah, find the bastard who did the deed." I put down the phone, a sour taste in my mouth from Tony's way of saying thank you. I could see how police departments went bad when the aggravation with each other became unbearable. Pretty soon the case was less important than getting someone off your back.

Pasquin nudged my back. "Let's go, m'lady. You got me up early; let's find some water." Pasquin had donned his familiar costume, including the battered straw hat.

We returned to the landing by river, Pasquin guiding his boat carefully through tall cypress trees into the main part of river, where deep and furious currents ran. He knew these currents and managed to make it feel as though we were gliding on perfectly calm water. At the landing, Pasquin stayed on board, leaning back with his hat over his eyes. "Hurry up," he mumbled.

I had to return to the house, then drag my gear back across soft, wet swamp ground. When I reached the boat, I lifted it gently to the floor. Pasquin peeked from under his hat. When I nudged him to sit up, he started up the boat and aimed it in the direction of the jutting bank. While he cleared the grass and pulled closer to clear water, I donned the flippers, mask and tank. Sitting atop the cave area, I rolled backward and hit the water, my skin cringing in shock from the frigid temperature. In a few seconds, I adjusted to the cold, turned downward, and swam toward the bottom of the bank.

The limestone near the opening was clear of eel grass, but the sides felt slick, almost slimy, not at all like the rough edges of the deep caves in Palmetto Springs. I swam around the opening, feeling for anything unnatural, anything that indicated a human presence.

Disappointed, I groped inside the dark entrance, risking injury and damning myself for forgetting to bring the light. The cave opening narrowed; I couldn't get more than three-fourths of my body inside. As I backed out slowly, the currents—not so strong here—pushed me gently from side to side. At one point, I miscalculated and bumped against an edge that poked almost directly outward from the wall. It was limestone, just like the rest of the cave, but it formed the shape of a club—a perfect place to tether something.

I surfaced, peeled off my mask, and said to Pasquin. "There's nothing there now, but I'll bet somebody has been using it."

"You mean I've got up with the chickens and batted mosquitoes all morning for nothing?" Pasquin revved the motor.

I laughed. "You're letting Tony Amado wear off on you, old man."

I spent the rest of the day puttering among the ruins of my house, nailing down loose boards in the kitchen wall, scrubbing one side of the living room to make painting easier, then sweeping—the infernal sweeping that has gone on in swamp houses ever since man decided to set up abodes here. The damp, black sand never entirely dries out when it's trampled inside; it sticks to the boards. Every day, the broom gets a hard workout, trying to push the stuff back out to the elements.

When darkness came, I sat on my clean porch and waited for the swamp to draw toward me as it did every evening. I remembered sitting here with Daddy after my mother died, sitting and rocking, trying to keep the chair going as fast as he did in spite of my short legs that wouldn't reach the floor. I wanted to turn on a light when I could no longer see the river, but Daddy said no.

"Listen. Listen to the voices out there," he said. "You're a part of that, too. Let the animals surround you, sing their lullabies to a sweet little human child. You know, our talking is like their calls and clicks. They're only communicating just like we are."

"But I'm afraid they'll come in and get me."

"Afraid? Do you think they're saying 'Hey! Cricket people,

there's this little human up on that porch. Let's hop up there and eat her up'?"

"Of course not! A cricket can't eat me." Then we laughed, and calm swept over me. The crickets weren't out to eat me, because they weren't capable. Besides, if they were, I had Daddy. He would see that they kept their distance.

Sadness washed over me when I realized the finality of death, that Daddy would no longer take care of me. He was in the ground now, closer to the crickets than I was. I trudged upstairs and crawled into bed. The curtains blew inward with a warm breeze that caressed my skin. I had the feeling of being gently rocked to sleep, of being one with the forest and unafraid of anything the swamp could send my way. Just before I went into a deep sleep, I heard the rain gently patter outside, its natural rhythms lulling me into perfect peace.

At some point, I woke with a start to a thump! I thought it came from downstairs. After listening to the soothing rain and feeling the breezes across my belly, I decided it was all a dream, then drifted back into oblivion.

CHAPTER THIRTEEN

The thump was real. The lock had been forced on the wooden front door, pushed open far enough for someone to enter, and the screen had been cut down the middle. No raccoons this time.

In a panic, I tried the cell phone, first inside the house, then under a clearing in the oaks outside. I cursed the company for not erecting enough towers, then jumped in the Honda. Halfway to Palmetto Springs, I reached Tony.

Back at the house, he searched around outside the door while a deputy traipsed through the house with a finger print dusting kit.

"You know, this cell phone is worthless out here!" I tossed it to Tony.

"Not worthless in your car or some place where the tower picks up the signal." He tossed it back. "Keep it until you get this ramshackle place wired."

The deputy joined us outside. He swiped beading sweat off his forehead with a rumpled handkerchief. "You need a window unit in there, Miz Fogarty."

"I need wires to support the unit, deputy. Right now, it would only blow the fuses."

He nodded, pulled out his pad, and asked, "What all did you

lose?"

"Looks like my television, a portable radio, and my underwater watch," I said. "Maybe more, but that's all I found missing so far."

"Looks like a kid or an addict who needed stuff to sell," He said. "You need to get a new door, one with a metal lining and dead bolts."

"In fact, you need to move," Tony chimed in, his exasperation showing in his pace from one end of the porch to the other. "This place just isn't safe anywhere you look." He stopped short and pointed beneath the steps. "You got a damn snake under there!"

"The snake didn't break in." I watched him to make sure he didn't whip out his pistol and shoot the creature.

"I'll get somebody to call Bailey Construction, see if we can't get them started on turning this place into a fortress." He tossed up his hands and walked off to use the patrol car radio.

I didn't want him to see my tears of frustration. To remodel the place and live amongst the trees next to the river had been my dream for years. Now, my humble boards were the pitiful victim of a petty thief.

Vernon stood on the dock. He wore only a swimsuit and a wide grin. Loman, beside him, in sport coat, tie, khaki pants, mopped sweat from his sleepy eyes.

"Where's Amado?" I asked.

"He'll get here soon enough." I turned to Vernon who winked at me. "You ready to dive?"

"Just a minute," interrupted Loman. "I've got some important news." Before he could tell us, he looked up.

Tony's car pulled up near the hotel. Loman took off, passing the Palmetto Sporting truck where two men checked tanks. Only two uniform cops stood duty outside the tapes.

"Amado tells me you've got a phone." Vernon stood close, teasing me with his half-naked body.

"Cellular. You'd like the number?"

He grinned even wider, and I marveled at how those white teeth and wide mouth lit up his whole face.

"Write the number on your slate, but don't expect to get me. I live in limbo, it seems."

He pulled his underwater slate from his bag and jotted down the number.

"You have anything else interesting in there?" I made small talk to keep him smiling at me.

He leaned over and began to pull items from the bag. "Paperweight I found in the ocean off Pensacola. An old letter opener. Somebody told me it looks Spanish. Solid brass handles off an old wreck, and believe it or not, a video. I doubt it's any good, but I'll let it dry out and see if it works. Probably kill my VCR."

"Where did you find it?" I said.

"Inside a wreck like all the other things. Only this wreck wasn't too old."

"I'll bet the lab boys can find something on it, even if your player can't."

Tony arrived on the dock with Loman who had given up trying to keep the sweat from his forehead. It dripped down his cheeks like tears. I wanted to tell him to take off the coat, but then he would have been out of uniform and out of macho sanctuary.

"We've got some evidence about Angie Stephoulous you

117

ought to hear," said Tony. "Loman's been tracking the interstate from Beaumont in the event the missing old lady is Delia Twiggins." He motioned for Loman to continue.

"Seems she was headed this way to reunite with her sister, says one of her church friends. The sister here—Carmina—told her about her heart problem, and in the end, Delia decided to give up her place and come live with her sister in the old family home. Anyhow, Delia got off the I-10 at a gas station and cafe outside of Pensacola. One of the waitresses remembered her. That's because another woman, a young, foreign-looking woman, sat near her and struck up a conversation. Seems the young lady's boyfriend got a little rough, and she wanted a ride back to Tallahassee. The two took off together. Waitress also identified the photo of the Stephoulous girl."

"So Angie Stephoulous and Delia Twiggins can be placed together just before they died?" I asked.

"Before Angie died. We don't know where Delia is, remember?"

"You've got her photos. Won't that hold up in court?"

"Probably, since we've got another body. But to hold court, we've got to have an arrested criminal."

"You got a motive?" asked Vernon, his smile now a serious thin line.

"None. Unless it's those silver dollars. We searched again, but no sign of them." Tony wrinkled his forehead.

"Look," Loman turned to me, "you don't suppose the old man—Pasquin—took them when you two were in the house?"

"If he did, he would have said something. He's not dishonest," I bristled.

"But," Tony added, "you did say he had an old box filled with them in his house, plus some in a bank."

"You're saying the ones in his house could be Carmina's?" Vernon looked at me, then at Tony.

"Well, I'm sure going to ask him," said Tony. "You two ready to dive?"

"What about my house? Who's taking care of things there?"

"I got a promise of four or five construction people. One of them I know personally. You'll have a house when you get out of here, maybe even a door and a roof." He pointed to the diving equipment like a teacher telling her students to get on with it.

The icy spring water washed away the hot sun. Vernon and I swam to the main cave, where I had found Delia. Running my hand over the limestone, I hoped to find transparent fishing line used for a tether. Nothing but crumbles fell between my fingers, like underwater snow. We scouted the cave as far as we dared, but neither of us wanted to go far back into the dark holes. We shone our lights into them, only to meet darkness a few feet beyond the beams. Body and evidence had drifted far into the blackness, or neither existed down here anymore. We swam out of the main cave, then made a quick check at the entrances of the others. The spring was pristine again, free from death and defilement.

Topside, we basked in the sun that rewarmed our blood. We lay on towels along the narrow sand beach and stared up at the tops of cyprus trees.

"Vernon, how well do you know Jack Ellison?"

"Not too well. He's the newest member of the diving team. Why?"

"Don't you guys have to go through some kind of rigorous training and testing before they hire you?" I sat up when two horseflies found my thighs appetizing.

"The most rigorous you can imagine, and we're constantly training," he said.

"Then why would he do those stupid things when we were down there? Stirring up sand to create a blind, swimming into a cave alone? That's not what I'd call good training."

"He knows better." Vernon sat up and swiped at a gnat that flew near his eyes. "It sounds deliberate. Is that what you're saying?"

I nodded. "He carried his diving bag down that day. Probably full of evidence bags, slates, lights—things we'd need down there, maybe. But I didn't see inside it. Maybe there were other things. It's too bizarre," I paused. "I'd really like to look into his diving bag."

"If he had anything hidden there, it would be out by now, right?" Vernon slapped himself on his bald pate. "Damn critters!"

"I'd still like to see inside."

A uniformed officer joined us. "Ms. Fogarty, Amado says to tell you Mr. Pasquin got burglarized last night, too. Seems they took his television and coffee maker. Tried to take the motor off the boat, but it must have been too heavy. Anyhow, he says to tell you they got clear prints off your door and off Mr. Pasquin's door."

"Is Pasquin all right?"

"Seems so. He slept through it all, just like you did."

"I've got to get home, Vernon. I need to check the work going on there, and I ought to see Pasquin. He's not young, you know."

"Tomorrow night?" He grinned, and I melted.

My peaceful kingdom had turned into a nest of trucks, boards, saws, dirty men, and one battered Volkswagen. My heart pounded as I parked under the trees. The workers used the carport area, but it wasn't Bailey Construction that made me nervous. That Volkswagen was too familiar—brown, full of leather bags, new seat covers. He was sitting out front when I walked around a pickup truck.

"Harry MacAllister! What are you doing on my steps?"

There he was, my old diving and bed partner, sitting with his chin in his hands like waiting for an old friend. He wore the familiar jeans and plaid shirt with the sleeves rolled up. His thick salt-and-pepper hair fell onto his forehead and curled over his ears. The Arizona sun had kept up his tan.

"I drove into town last night. Tony said you had a phone number, but he wouldn't give it to me. Said he'd have to get your permission first."

"Good for him!" I walked past him and stomped onto the porch. "And you'd better not sit there. I have a guardian snake under my porch."

"Can't we talk?" He sounded whiny.

The anger in the pit of my stomach rose, and I knew I'd better calm down before I faced him. "I'm tired. There'll be no talking tonight."

"Tomorrow night, then?"

"I've got a date!"

The hammering and saws fell silent. I realized the workers had stopped to hear the quarrel. Turning around, I went through my new door and headed upstairs, almost stepping in the gap at the top. I slammed the bathroom door and waited. Finally, I heard the Volkswagen engine start up and leave my swamp.

"Ma'am?" A male voice called up the stairs. I opened the

door and peeked out to see a scraggly man, his thin hair falling nearly to his shoulders. Scratches spotted his bare, gaunt arms. Wormy—that's what the old-timers would call him. He jerked his shoulders like electricity hit him at intervals.

"Boss says you need a stair repaired in here?"

I motioned to the missing step near the top. He hauled up his tool box and some boards. I hadn't planned to watch him, but I had the feeling of seeing him somewhere before. "Excuse me, but do I know you?"

He looked up, his eyes, rheumy blue and yellow, almost disappeared from view. I got the feeling of a startled rabbit about to run.

"I think you came over to the Seafood Company the other day. You were talking to Mr. Petroulious."

"You work there?"

"Sometimes I do odd jobs for Arno—Mr. Petroulious. Mostly, I work in construction." He made a short, hard sniff and jerked his head in a nervous tic.

I wondered if Arno Petroulious owned the construction company along with the restaurant and seafood operations.

"I'm Luanne Fogarty, and you are?"

"Joe Bandy, ma'am. I know who you are. They named this little town after your family, right?"

"Right. Well, Joe, do a good job on that step. I've almost broken my neck on it twice." I stepped back into the bedroom and closed the door.

Looking out my window, I saw males, sweaty and tattooed. Most wore cotton bandanas tied around stringy-hair foreheads. By the end of the day, their faces would be ashy white at the top and blistered red at the bottom. One man in a dirty tank top glanced up and met my stare—Zull! So the man looking for gas in the middle of the night really was a construction worker!

I planned to stay in motion the rest of the day. Low on supplies, I wanted to drive to the Publix beyond Palmetto Spring. I also had to see Pasquin. Maybe I'd treat him to Mama's Table.

Pasquin steered us in his boat to Mama's Table. The sky went from fine white streaks over blue to pale blue streaks over purple. The river turned black under the sunset, and cypress trees outlined themselves against the sky.

"Harry came back." I said it matter of factly, after we ordered.

"Most men stray every once in a while. Most come back." He made a slurping sound of appreciation when his fried oyster plate arrived.

"I can't accept him after the way he left. I'm not the forgiving kind."

"Scratch his eyes out, scream bloody murder at him, but take him back. He needs you now. You'll forgive him if you want to."

"And if I don't want to? What if I've found someone else?" I twirled my fork in cheese grits.

"Now that's the best medicine for a wandering male. Get yourself another. Make him jealous as hell!" He sat back and chuckled.

I realized then that the Cajun philosophy of life, especially the old one, would not jibe with my liberated woman style.

"You ever been married, Pasquin?" I pointed at him with a fried shrimp.

"Many times—in God's eyes. Never said the vows for the priest though, preacher neither." He grinned at me. "You should have seen this old fool when he was young. Strong muscles from pushing them cargo crates around on them barges. Women used to goggle-eye me with my shirt off. Indecent back then, and when their mamas caught them, whoo boy!" He popped an oyster into his mouth.

"I'll bet you got a few behind meal sacks on those barges."

"A few, a few. Yes-siree!" Two more oysters disappeared down his throat.

A sudden thought picked at my brain, and I wanted to ask about my mother, but I pushed it away.

"Pasquin, did Tony ask you about those silver dollars?" I tried to be serious and picked up a shrimp with my fork. It didn't fit my mouth that way; I slid the thing off the tines and consumed it, minus the tail.

"Did. Peeved me a little when he suggested mine were taken from Carmina's house. Told him like I told you. I keep a box of them around for emergencies. In case I run out of cash. I never had to use them. What do you suppose happened to Carmina's?"

I shook my head. "Did you know that Delia had decided to come and live with Carmina?"

"No, but Miss Kah-meena didn't confide in me much. Kinda got mad at me a few years ago when I wouldn't take up with a widow friend of hers. But I didn't marry when I was young and vee-rile. Sure not going to do it when I'm old and flaccidly in-clined."

I laughed out loud. What Pasquin lacked in male potency, he made up for in verbal acrobatics. He would make some old lady a fine companion, but with that house of his, it shouldn't be a live-in companion. Would I be his female counterpart in twenty-five years? The old woman of the swamps, the one with a snake under her doorsteps?

Our key lime pie arrived at the same time a uniformed deputy opened the door and spied us.

"Been looking for you, ma'am. Amado says you better meet him at that hunt camp down the river."

CHAPTER FOURTEEN

The deputy offered to drive me to the site, but Pasquin's boat would get me there quicker.

"We might be out late," I said as he asked the waitress to bundle up the pie.

"Don't you know Cajuns sit up half the night, woman?"

"Okay! You can nap in the boat. Let's go!"

We tied up next to a police boat, its radio blasting with calls every few minutes. Crowds of men gathered farther up the incline, near the trailer slabs.

Pasquin pulled his hat over his face. "I'm resting right here. You go on up."

"Do you think you could listen for any interesting tidbits of information coming over that radio?"

"If I'm awake."

I moved up the hill where Amado conversed with Zull, and Loman circled a slab of broken cement. Zull looked away from me when I met his eyes.

"Fellows couldn't get this slab even no matter what they tried. Then the hook-ups wouldn't match just right. They gave up and decided to start all over. The other slabs were fine. Something went wrong with this one. That's when they came and got me." Zull looked at me, a silent explanation of why he wasn't still on my roof. "I started to break up the cement and when a hand popped up, I called you guys." He had removed his tank top, exposing red-blotched flab.

"Who broke up the rest of this?" Tony pointed to chunks of cement thrown onto the sides of the slab.

"One of the guys thought it might be a fake hand someone put there as a joke. He said we ought to pull up some more to see if it was real." He made a gesture toward an uneven chunk, covered in cement dust.

I moved closer, next to Loman, and stared at the crude rectangle. Through the dust, a human shape took form. Hardened cement had settled in the eyes and mouth. I recognized the outline of eyeglasses around the neck.

"It's Delia Twiggins!" I said in a half whisper.
Loman turned to me and nodded. "But we'll have to pull her out and do tests to be sure. Got to get Mr. Pasquin to identify her, too."

"He's down there in his boat. But he hasn't seen her in a long time," I said.

"He is the next of kin—if it's really her. Where the hell is the crime scene unit!" Tony slapped the sides of his trousers.

A uniformed cop produced some yellow tape, and Loman helped him stake it around the trailer slab.

"We need to see everyone on this job." Tony gave the order to Zull.

"Okay, I'll round them up. I left two at the lady's house. Two more are off today. Joe Bandy," he pointed to the jerky man with watery eyes, "been here off and on. His job is to start up the cement mixer before we get here in the mornings. It was running this a.m."

Bandy, who fixed my step, had been inside my house and

knew the layout.

Pasquin had to trudge up the hill and look at another dead relative. The two of us stood quietly, staring down at Delia's broken-rock grave. She looked like a statue from medieval times, one that had been discarded by the sculptors as imperfect.

The crime scene techs pushed everyone back and went to work. It was ironic, dusting dust for prints. Neither the techs nor the coroner would touch the body, not even with gloved hands because the fine cement powder took on the shape of anything placed there. Eventually, the crime scene people would transport the body to Tallahassee where they would clean her up.

"Moving her won't be easy," said one tech. "Besides the hard cement on her dead limbs, she's full of scars where the hammers and picks pulled material from her skin. Might be hard to tell who did what."

Other techs tagged chunks of cement to be transported to the lab and searched for pieces of flesh as well as prints.

Tony finished his interviews and came over to speak to Pasquin about identification.

"I can't tell from this stuff," said Pasquin, his leather-brown face grown ashen from the sight.

"Then go home and wait for the call," said Tony. "You can look at her when she's cleaned up. Luanne will drive you into Tallahassee."

I followed Pasquin back to his boat. He moved faster than usual, ready to run from scenes that disturbed his universe.

"Harry is back." Tony said, as we walked away.

"No kidding!" I noticed a slight grin on his face when I turned away.

The paved road to Tallahassee was strewn with dead armadillos every few miles. Neither Pasquin nor I made our usual morbid comments. The sight of death—stiff, squashed, rotten—was a reminder of the indignity of a violent killing.

"I'm not looking forward to this," Pasquin said.

"It should last only a few seconds. Just take a deep breath, do it, then turn around and leave. They're going to want to talk to you a little about her, but don't let them do it in the room with the body. They're so used to death, they sometimes forget to respect the living."

At the morgue, Pasquin took my advice. I watched him give a quick glance when the coroner pulled the sheet off the face. Somebody had closed her eyes, but the mouth was still slightly open. Only a fine dusting, like face powder, remained on her skin. The hair was visible now, though still caked in places with hardened cement. Pasquin left the room, shaking his head. The coroner wheeled the gurney into another room. I joined Loman and Pasquin in the hallway.

"Poor Delia. Never saw her like that before." He looked at his feet and kept shaking his head.

"We'll notify the Beaumont police. Is there any other family?" Loman took notes in a small pad.

"Doubtful. Don't think she ever married, unless she did it in secret. No kids that I know of." Pasquin fanned with his hat, in spite of the frigid air inside the building.

We returned to Fogarty Spring in silence. I thought maybe Pasquin wanted to be alone with the past, to remember happier days with his two girl cousins. He surprised me when he suddenly lifted his head and talked about the burglary.

"Took my coffee maker, damn kid!" He slapped his hat down on his knees and left it there.

"How do you know it was a kid?"

"Kids take things like that to sell, maybe to buy drugs."

"Don't adults do the same?"

"Not around here. Maybe some drifter, but folks in these parts—even if they are poor—will work an odd job or go for a Salvation Army handout, but steal things, never. Most older folks wouldn't know where to sell them anyway."

I didn't want to disagree with Pasquin, to remind him that most of the older folk weren't nearly as old as he.

He took a deep breath when we arrived in front of my house. "I'm going fishing, Luanne. Fishing makes me forget about bad things. Guess that's why I've worked on the river all my life."

I said goodbye and watched him disappear down the path, then I headed inside.

I felt out of sorts, pestered—as Daddy used to say, or was it Pasquin? I changed into a suit and headed for the landing through trees. Stepping on damp pine needles, I kept a watch out for snakes. At the tree line, the needles turned to mulch in the black sand, then mud, and finally shallow water. These were gator rests, where they stowed their decaying meals in a few inches of water, and where I kept a vigil for any signs of their gray hide. Lately, children had taken up throwing food in the water. They liked to watch the gator eyes move above the surface, then the jaws splash up to grab the chunks of bread and wieners. Rangers placed signs throughout the tourist areas to warn people against this; "AN ALLIGATOR DOESN'T KNOW YOU FROM THE FOOD YOU ARE THROWING," they screamed in bright orange lettering on a black background. Nor did the alligator know where the tourist areas ended and the rest of the river began. Twice last summer in Florida, children playing near water had been clamped in prehistoric jaws and dragged to watery deaths. I didn't want to be taken for walking food.

Leaving my towel and sandals on the broken dock, I eased into the river. The water here was not nearly as cold as in the springs, and water grass blinded me to the bottom. But I didn't worry about gators. They rarely bother a swimmer unless you step on them or disturb their babies. Water moccasins were another matter, but in the forty-plus years I had been swimming here, I'd never come upon one in the water.

I lay on my back and gently pushed myself into clear water, feeling the temperature drop as I went. The sun blasted down from a cloudless sky. I closed my eyes and let the water cool me. When my face grew too hot, I turned over and cooled my front, holding my head to the side just enough to breathe. Finally, I dived into the depths, letting the gentle current wash over me. At this spot, I could see the bottom, could swim all the way down, pick up tiny snails, and return without gasping for breath. A few feet away, the current picked up, and any swimmer would have a hard time staying in one place. Farther out, the bottom dropped. The cave I had tried to search lay under the bank that jutted into the river. I may have been in control of my safety for the moment, but on this river, one was always on the edge of danger.

A familiar voice called from the landing. "You'll grow a fishtail and turn into a mermaid if you stay in there too long."

"Harry!" I didn't know what else to say. My only escape was underwater.

"Please, just hear me out. I'm not asking for anything. Besides, Amado has a job for us."

"I have a diving partner." I felt the heat rise behind my neck in spite of the cold water.

"So I've heard. I still need to talk. Come on up." He held out his hand. I swam to the dock but refused his help, climbing up the large rusty nails placed there years ago for a ladder.

"All right, talk." I dried my hair and turbaned my head with the towel.

"The thing in Arizona didn't work out, but then I guess you can see that."

"I don't see anything. What does that have to do with me?"

"Everything. I admit I got the hots for—her, you know..."

"Men always have the hots for 'you know.' Cut it out! You chased her to Arizona, leaving me with a phone message. Now what else is there to say?" I leaned against a dock post, refusing to join him in a sitting position.

"She had a thing for a couple of other guys out there, and the lecture position didn't pan out. It was just a summer replacement job I didn't want. I ended up having to take a leave of absence here—without pay." He squinted against the sun, playing the pitied child with his eyes.

I wanted to laugh. "So she collects archeologists, and you decided not to offer yourself as part of the display."

"I'm not carrying a torch for her. That feeling died out about the time we arrived in the desert." He shaded his eyes from the sun. "I did miss you, though. I spent most of the time asking myself why I ever left."

"What? No dinosaur bones, ancient sea whale ribs, remains of space aliens in that desert?" I felt myself getting teary, my anger boiling into resentment.

"I never even looked." He lowered his head like a mischievous child.

"It can't be like it was before. I trusted you. You betrayed that trust, and I just can't brush my resentment aside. I've spent

132

the last few months getting over you. And, I'm not exactly dissatisfied with the next guy in my life."

"Vernon?"

"God! Word does get out."

"No, it's not out. I asked Tony if you were seeing anyone. He thought something was going on between you two."

"Yeah, well, it's in the infant stage, but I'm not ready to cut it off."

His voice lowered, "I'm not asking you to resume where we left off. If we could just be professional friends again, we could see where we go with our feelings. I won't lie and say I don't feel a little jealous when you're with Vernon, but just don't eliminate me with your anger. Give it time to cool, and then we'll see what happens."

I looked at Harry, his full head of wavy hair a big contrast to Vernon's bald pate. It dawned on me that hair was about the only physical difference. Their diving kept them in good muscle tone and constant tan. In the back of my mind, I realized they even moved similarly in bed.

"If Tony has a job for us, I'll work with you—and Vernon, if it involves diving. I may trust you underwater, but nowhere else."

He followed me off the landing, but I didn't invite him inside. He didn't drive away immediately. When I had climbed to the second floor, I peeked through the upstairs curtains, and watched him walk to his Volkswagen, head bowed and shoulders slumped. *Damn! Men have this pity thing down to an art!*

I was absorbed in painting my new door when Zull arrived on foot. He had parked somewhere on the rutted road, afraid to bring the heavy truck any farther into the swamp.

"Sorry, ma'am, but we'll be back here in full force tomorrow. Cops shut down the hunt camp work until they search every inch of the place. We ought to be able to finish that roof in a few days provided it don't rain buckets. Like your new door?"

"It's fine. I'm surprised you didn't have to build a new frame, though. It's heavy for this old house."

"We shored up the frame a little, but it's pretty sturdy. Fact is, this old house has some sturdy parts still. Somebody built it with good stuff. Of course, you have some areas that ain't worth fixing." He scraped mud from his shoe on the bottom step.

"Zull, who owns Bailey Construction?"

"Old man Petroulious. Owns fish markets, two, three construction companies, even a big fishing boat. He owns the hunt camp, too."

He stayed in one spot, watching me paint until I grew uncomfortable with his presence. I turned and tried to find an expression that would say to either continue the conversation or leave.

"Ma'am?" He sounded humble, like Harry.

"Yes?"

"You see Joe Bandy out here this morning?"

"Here?" I kept on painting.

"We can't find him, and the cops suspect he stole some things from you and some other people who live back in this swamp. If that's true, we need to get rid of him. But, we can't find him right now." Zull heard a sound in the bushes and turned from side to side in a sudden jerk.

"Well, I sure don't know where he is." I stopped painting and thought about my television.

"If he shows up, could you give me a call?" He handed over

a torn sheet of paper with a number written on it. "He's got some of our tools, and we need them back."

His hand trembled as I took the paper from him. I shook, too, with anger, thinking again how Bandy knew the inside of my house.

Zull walked back down the path. I left the door ajar to dry, then headed upstairs. I automatically stopped at the place where the missing stair had been, now repaired in shiny new wood. Maybe Joe Bandy went on a binge and sometimes didn't show up to work, but he was one hell of a carpenter.

CHAPTER FIFTEEN

Do things strike other people at three in the morning? I awoke suddenly to rain pounding on the roof. Maybe the sound of water made me remember the blown-up photos of Delia. I needed to see the one of that thing attached to her wrist. It reminded me of a Bible, the kind with a zip-up cover they gave me when I attended summer Bible school as a child.

Sitting on my porch, sipping coffee, I tried to put things together. The predawn morning lent itself to thinking. Crickets and frogs had given up their nightly choir practice to find places to hide from the birds on breakfast forages. The forest around me slept as far as I could tell. Anything on the prowl moved without sound.

Delia Twiggins decides to heal the wounds with her sister. She stops at a cafe in Pensacola. Angie Stephoulous joins her and asks for a ride back to Tallahassee because she was pissed off with her boyfriend. Who was the boyfriend? Pensacola is near the coast—boats, docks, harbors. She worked for a seafood company. Boats, harbors, seafood, imports—drugs? Delia and Angie end up dead, both strangled, both bodies placed in the springs. And the bones we found. Is there a serial killer out there with an underwater fantasy? Frank Ellison worked with Angie, and he is a diver. So is his brother, Jack. Carmina has a heart problem. A neighbor finds her dead on her floor. Did she die the same time as Delia and Angie? Did something happen as a catalyst for this attack? Why did somebody deliberately move Delia's body in the spring? Because that someone knew it had been found, stupid! Who knew? The teens, Tony, Loman, the uniformed guards, maybe the hotel staff, surely the tour boat staff, possibly the entire sheriff's department. Did Jack Ellison know before he was called in from the Ochlockonee River boating accident? He could have. The men in the department talk freely about their jobs. The papers didn't print anything until the following day. At least one reporter knew a body had been found. And Carmina's boarder?

When I saw the sun coming through the trees, I drove to the Palmetto Hotel and phoned Tony. He nursed a buzz in his head from staying awake too long.

"You want that picture blown up further?" I heard him gulp coffee. "Can't you wait until after breakfast?"

I ignored him. "That thing tied around Delia's wrist, I don't know how clear it is, but it's in the full-body photo. Can you get the lab to blow up just that part?"

"You know," he hesitated, "come to think of it, we didn't find it when they dug her out of the cement. I'll check with the lab. And, yeah, I'll get them to enhance the photo. Any more orders?"

"I've got two questions: Why was Angie going to Pensacola, and were all three women killed around the same time?"

"Died. Carmina had a heart attack, remember?"

"Yeah, well a shock could have caused that attack, like seeing her sister killed. Her body wouldn't have to be hidden because she died of natural causes." I hesitated. "Might as well add a third question. Where is Angie's car that she drove out of the parking lot when they last saw her?"

"Okay. We're asking the same questions, including how they got to the springs if they were murdered at Carmina's house." He remained silent a moment, then added, "And before you think about more questions, there had to be somebody who knew scuba diving to place the bodies in the caves. That limits the field considerably."

"Any word on the blood you found in Carmina's house?"

Tony grunted a no. "My head is gonna burst."

"Okay, one more. Besides the missing silver dollars, was anything else taken?"

"There was no money in the women's purses. You saw the house. It hadn't been totally ransacked." He sighed. "For now, we're calling the motive as robbery."

I put down the phone. Would someone kill, then go to the trouble of placing the bodies in deep water caves, just for a little cash?

Pasquin had to return to Tallahassee to take care of some paperwork on Delia, and to talk to the Beaumont authorities. I volunteered to drive him. Zull and his roofers, minus Joe Bandy, arrived early and started pounding. I welcomed the escape.

"You think I'm going to have to ride over to Beaumont, Luanne?" Pasquin fanned himself even in the air-conditioned car. His nervousness at dealing with family matters matched my restlessness at wanting to see that blown-up photo.

"I'll drive you if you have to go. I'd like to see where she lived." I placed my hand on Pasquin's hat and pushed it gently to his knees.

Loman met us in a drab room with beige plastic chairs, an iron-gray table with a gash in one end, and a uniformed officer with a lap computer. "Suspect did that." He pointed to the gash. "We leave it there to remind us to do body searches."

"This is a homicide case, Mr. Pasquin, and if you don't mind, we'll sit in on the discussion you have with the Beaumont people in case something comes to light." Loman's half-opened eyes questioned Pasquin.

"Just can't understand why my family is in such a mess all of a sudden." He looked at me, then placed his hat on the table.

We waited ten minutes. Three men in suits came in and shook hands with Loman. Two were Beaumont police, one a lawyer from Delia's bank. He pulled out a large envelope and placed it in front of him.

Loman put a tape recorder on the table. He read our names and titles into the recorder, then made a statement that the tape was being made in conjunction with the Palmetto Springs murder case. After citing the case number, he nodded for the bank lawyer to begin.

"Miss Delia Twiggins," he spoke stiffly, "owned her condo free and clear. She sold it on June first for $75,000. She deposited the money in an account with us, where she already had a small savings account of $15,678. On June thirty, she withdrew $2,000 in traveler's checks, telling the bank clerk, whom she had known for a considerably long time, that she was moving to Florida, back to her family home. To date, the money she left in those accounts is still there. Her will leaves any worldly goods she has at the time of her demise to the Library Society. There is no mention of family."

"What was her connection to the Library Society?" Loman asked without looking at the man.

"She was a retired city librarian. Most of her life was spent in that field. I guess she wanted to give them something when she left. They do put up plaques in the local library when people make large charitable contributions."

"Do you want to ask any questions, Mr. Pasquin?"

Pasquin jumped slightly. He looked confused. "Why would somebody want to kill her and do her body like that?"

"I'll have to acquiesce to these gentlemen," said the bank lawyer.

The Beaumont detectives ran the gamut of questions about Delia and her sister, their feud, her possible—however remote—associations with criminal sorts. Pasquin shook his head in bewilderment. He had no answers. His Beaumont cousin was someone from his past, a total stranger in the present. His Tallahassee cousin didn't fare much better.

"Are you acquainted with a Mr. Quinlan Rentell?" Pasquin shook his head again.

"We've checked out Rentell's alibis. He wasn't in town that week." Loman spoke, but still didn't look at the men.

When they left the sheriff's office, neither the men from Beaumont nor those in Tallahassee knew any more about their citizen's demise than they did before they arrived. No mention was made of Pasquin traveling to Texas. The wear on his nerves from the murders took a toll on the elderly man, and he dealt with it by fanning himself until we sat in the Honda on the way home.

"I don't know how you live without air-conditioning in that old house," he said. "It don't have insulation at all." He rambled on about my house, how it wasn't natural for a smart young woman to want to live in the woods, spraying night and day for mosquitoes, nailing broken boards together, and stepping over poisonous animals. He didn't want a response. I kept my mouth shut until we reached my place. A patrol car was parked under a tree, a uniformed officer knocking at my door.

"Okay, old man. If I didn't live in this old house, you'd be riding in one of those cars." I opened the door and headed for the porch.

"We found the kid that broke into your house, ma'am," said the officer. "Yours, too, Mr. Pasquin. He lives across the river. Been in trouble off and on for two years. Left his prints everywhere, and he's still got some of the stuff. Tried to sell it. That's how we caught him." The man's face lit up in a grin when he stopped talking.

Pasquin's face smiled back at him. "Maybe now things will start going the other way," he said. He sat in a porch rocker and fanned himself, "and maybe I'll get my coffee pot back."

"Sir, could you and Ms. Fogarty come by the Palmetto Springs office and identify your articles?" The cop seemed out of another era, his training almost too polite. I knew he could probably shoot right through someone's heart, but he wasn't going to upset anyone.

"Come on, Pasquin," I said. "Let's go do that, then get a bite to eat at the hotel there, if they're still serving."

They were serving. In fact, the park had been reopened and a glass bottom boat moved slowly around the spring, its microphoned tour echoing across the swamp. Pasquin and I sat in the grand room, heavy crystal lights hanging over us, elegant drapes flowing around the floor-to-ceiling windows with their half oval tops. Ladies in crisp white aprons rolled carts of food around to the tables, taking care to serve, family style, bowls of fried okra, grits, and field peas in Southern fashion. I was the youngest diner in the room, Pasquin possibly the oldest.

"You think that Macklin kid did those murders?" Pasquin referred to Sonny Macklin, the burglar who was caught trying to sell my television to Joe Bandy. Zull sent someone to look for Bandy when he didn't show up for work the second day. He found him at his swamp shack, drunk, and arguing about the price of the television. When Bandy freaked and ran the man off with a baseball bat, Zull called in the authorities.

"I guess it's possible," I said. "They're checking his alibis. He's what—sixteen? I guess he could have killed, but I don't want to think he did. From what Zull said, I suspect Bandy may have been in on the burglaries, told the boy what stuff was in my house. But, could that kid have deposited those bodies in the springs? No way. He doesn't know how to dive. Besides, who's going to kill for—what, a few silver dollars?"

Pasquin paused, his face staring somewhere in his past. "I knew a man once, killed for 'bout nothing. He worked on the riverboats with us. Strong man. Carried two crates, one on each shoulder." Pasquin leaned back and took hold of the chair arms. "Now, there was this new captain. Man liked to wear silver—belt buckles and hatband clips. He spent his spare time polishing the stuff. Lots of men talked about that silver, saying it would buy somebody his own boat." He looked at me. "If we had our own boat, we wouldn't be laboring for the man, see. Anyhow, this one big guy got a little whiskey in him one night and sneaked 'round to where the captain was sleepin' in his hammock. Sliced the man's throat. He didn't stop there. Sliced him up and dumped him overboard to the gators." Pasquin made a chuckling sound. "He done it so quiet, nobody woke up. We saw the blood next morning, and the big man was gone, so we figured he'd run off with the silver. Sure enough, they caught him halfway to Port St. Joe. Tried to use the silver to buy a boat."

"You're saying that a few dollars would be plenty of motive?"

"Yes, ma'am, money in any form is motive. Bible says that."

We sat with our peach cobbler and coffee, nibbling because

142

neither of us wanted to go back into the humidity, to houses where we had to serve ourselves. We watched as elderly diners filed out, paying their bills, pulling toothpicks from the tiny jar on the counter, then drifting into the hotel lobby. A few stopped to play checkers, but most went on to the parking lot and headed home. It was almost dark when Amado came into the room.

He approached the table in a sense of urgency, reflected in his clenched jaw. "I've been looking for you two. We've got a problem. Seems Joe Bandy got drunk, then a little mad at Zull who, he believes, put the cops onto him. Joe went over to your place, Luanne, with a baseball bat and poked Zull around a bit. Did a number on your windows, too." He looked away from me.

"Oh, damn! Where is he now?"

"We've got an APB out, but if he follows his usual pattern, he'll land in a ditch somewhere. He's a mean drunk. Been in jail more than once after a binge of bourbon and coke—the nose kind. I need you to follow me to your place."

"Is Zull still there?"

"In the hospital. We had to call an ambulance. Joe may be a little guy, but he's quick and strong when he's high."

Pasquin and I followed Tony's taillights down the paved road and through the swamp. When we pulled into the carport, we met a uniformed officer who told us to watch where we stepped. There was glass on the ground, big chunks of it.

"I planned to replace those old windows anyhow," I said as I looked at the one that faced onto the carport. Crumpled wood and jagged glass were all that remained of the sashes that had been there since before I was born. In the front, I found the same thing where shards of glass lay about the porch, even in the rock-

143

ing chairs. I also found blood on the gray boards.

"Zull was around back and up on a ladder," Tony said. "He heard the noise, came running around here where Joe took the bat to him. It had to be an element of surprise. Zull is three times the size of Joe."

I bent to remove some of the larger chunks of glass from the doorway. "You know, it seems the forces of the universe are telling me not to fix up this place."

"I've been telling you that," added Tony.

"Well, you and the forces can just go to Hell! I'm going ahead with it. Just tell me when you find Joe Bandy."

Car lights moved down the rutted road. We stood looking in their direction, anticipating trouble. A utility van pulled under the trees. When the door opened, Jack Ellison walked towards us. He smiled.

"I thought I'd check on this Joe Bandy thing. Boys at the station told me about the attack."

"What's your interest in Joe?" asked Tony.

"I arrested him once. He tried to steal some diving equipment from my brother. Man was so drunk, he could barely stand up without leaning on the patrol car. He got a sentence for drunk and disorderly, but the judge said he didn't think the man knew what he was stealing. He dropped the charge. I don't agree with that judge. I've heard Bandy talk about diving stuff and how good the money is for new equipment." Even in the porch light, Jack squinted like he did in the sun.

"We can't find him, but if we do, we'll let you know." Tony said.

Jack looked at his feet, unwilling to go back to his car. "Did Zull talk about Joe saying anything? I mean the man has some equipment of Frank's, I'm sure. But we've never been able to locate it. I'd like to know if he said anything to Zull."

"Why would he say anything about diving equipment while he was bashing someone's brains out?" asked Tony.

"Drunks say lots of things. You know that, Tony."

Something incensed Tony. I could see the jaws working over clenched teeth. "Ellison, I don't think he said anything about your equipment, but I'd sure like to see what it is that's missing. Sounds like a diamond-studded cylinder!"

Ellison backed off, said polite good-byes, and returned to his van. Tony stood frozen, staring at the taillights that finally disappeared into the trees. Turning to the uniformed cop, he snapped, "Tomorrow, first thing on my desk, I want to see the complaint Frank Ellison filed against Bandy. And, I want to know what kind of equipment he was supposed to have taken."

"Tony," I added, "if Bandy thought diving equipment was valuable, and he was in cahoots with Macklin, then why wasn't my cylinder taken in the burglary?"

CHAPTER SIXTEEN

Tony arrived in a foul mood. "I want you to accompany me to Ellison's house—Frank Ellison. I've got the complaint filed a while back against Joe Bandy, and I want to check out this equipment that's missing. I need a diver along to explain things."

After a long night of cleaning up glass, then nailing boards over windows, I wanted to sleep late. Instead, I hauled out, made coffee and nibbled on some store-bought cornbread muffins that tasted more like cake than bread.

"If this damn Jack Ellison is in some kind of trouble with his brother and embarrasses the department, I'll have his ass," said Tony. He drank coffee and paced the kitchen. Every few steps he stopped to run his finger across the patched screen.

"Where does Frank live?" I asked.

"On a spread not far from here. Can you speed it up?"

I retreated upstairs and pulled on jeans and a Palmetto Springs tee shirt, their reptilian issue. It sported a gator, a rattlesnake, and a frog.

Frank Ellison owned a farm on the other side of the river, almost directly opposite the hunt camp and three miles from the river's edge. Tony chose to take the bridge at Fogarty Spring, then turn down a narrow paved road, and finally to a dirt road that had been recently graded. Funny how Ellison got the county to do this for him.

The wide dirt road had deep ditches on each side, its red clay so hard that tire tracks were all but invisible. We drove out of the marshy river area. No reeds or water plants grew here. Instead, a pine forest lined the road on a slight incline all the way to the rambling, brown-shingled ranch house. A shiny new pickup truck, maroon and silver, stood near the front porch. Out buildings, some brand-new aluminum jobs, others the familiar gray boards of small sheds built at least twenty years ago, lined the periphery of the trees. They could have been small barns or storage facilities. A lone man with grizzly chin hairs that hadn't seen a shave for a week stopped clipping a hedge. He shifted the straps on his overalls.

I followed Tony out of the car.

"We'd like to see Mr. Frank Ellison," said Tony, flashing his sheriff's badge.

"He's not here at the moment. I'm sort of the caretaker. Can I help?" The man's eyes widened; his mouth gaped open, revealing missing teeth.

"I'm here about this complaint against a Joe Bandy." Tony held up the papers. "Seems the man took some diving equipment. Know anything about that?" Tony's eyes darted about the grounds.

"Lately? I don't think Mr. Ellison has been complaining about Bandy these past few days." The man tried to follow Tony's eyes.

"It's a few weeks old, but I have to check it out anyway." Tony's eyes darted from the house to the nearest barn. He wasn't a good liar. "I need to check his equipment, maybe to see if his complaint can be closed. I mean, maybe the equipment in the

147

complaint is here now." Tony turned to me. "This is Ms. Fogarty, a diving expert. She can identify the equipment."

The man put his clippers on the ground and rubbed his hands on the overalls. "Well, I guess I can show you the barn where he keeps that stuff." He hesitated for a moment, then motioned us to follow him.

We passed the first barn, the largest hulk on the property. I could see between the worn gray boards; it housed a tractor and another truck. The second barn, smaller but better built, had the brown hue of newer lumber. A generator stood outside the door; shiny metal revealed its newness. The man glanced at Tony, then pulled a key chain from his pocket and unlocked the double doors. Tony waited for him to open them all the way back, then followed him inside.

"We don't want anyone to say we broke into this place," he whispered to me as we passed through the double doors.

"New tanks over there, old ones over here. Air containers in that corner. Most of the masks and flippers are over there." He stood aside and watched me examine twelve old cylinders, rusty with broken gauges. There were three new cylinders, well maintained and stored correctly. The old ones leaned against one wall.

Tony made a pretense of asking about the accessories hanging from specially-made hooks around the walls. I returned to the old tanks. No one would want these—except maybe for scrap. I kneeled close and ran my fingers across the rusty sections. Near the top of each one, I found a pencil mark going clear round, as though someone had measured, then marked them.

I nodded to Tony and, without calling attention to myself, showed him the marks.

Tony pointed to the new tanks and said, "Says here in the complaint that Bandy took one large cylinder, and a few tools. Do you know if these tanks are the only ones Mr. Ellison has?"

The man shrugged. "He uses them for diving, and never lets them get in bad condition. Said nothing is worse than a tank going bad down deep in the ocean."

"He does ocean diving?" I asked.

"With the Seafood Company, yes ma'am."

"He never dives in the lakes and springs around here?"

"The company works only salt waters as far as I know. They get the fresh water fish from some outfit up in Georgia."

"Then all his tanks are accounted for?" Tony was fishing for something.

"Yeah, except maybe the real old ones. They come in, then go out again. Says he sells them to scrap yards."

"Where does he get the old tanks?" I asked again.

"Finds them in garage sales, old sporting shops, even on the bottom of the ocean sometimes. Loads them in here, cuts them up, then gets rid of them. I guess he makes money off the things."

"And those are his cutting tools?" I pointed to a machine that had a motor at one end, some intricate sawing pieces at the other.

He shrugged. "Don't know. I never come in here except to deliver messages or beer. He's got some men who help him with the old tanks."

"Does Joe Bandy ever help?" Tony asked.

"Yeah. He does when he's sober. Can't always keep him that way."

Tony and I glanced at each other. Bandy seemed to have been a fixture in a lot of places.

"Is Mr. Ellison married?" Tony's question jarred me.

"Nope. Was once, I think, why?"

"Just wondered if there was a wife we could leave a message

with."

"Leave it with me, if you like." The man held out a calloused hand.

"Just tell him we inquired about the complaint, and unless we hear otherwise from him, we'll close it."

In the car on the way back to the house, I wondered about those pencil marks around the tanks. And those cutting tools. Was someone cutting up the tanks right there on the property? If all he was doing was selling them for scrap, he didn't need to cut them.

"Tony," I asked, breaking into the hum of the air conditioner, "if this complaint is old, and Ellison really hasn't lost anything, why did Jack Ellison make the effort to find out what Bandy said during his rampage?"

"Just what I was thinking. I need to talk to Jack. Want to be in on this?"

I nodded. He turned the car around and headed for Tallahassee.

Jack Ellison fidgeted on the metal chair in Tony's office. He avoided eye contact with either of us. "Forget it. I guess I jumped the gun on this one," he said.

"Look, you showed up at Luanne's house to find out what Bandy said. Why should we forget that?"

"Listen, a few weeks ago, Frank caught Bandy rummaging through his truck, then again through his storage barn. Some tanks went missing; at least that's what he thought. Frank got hot under the collar and called me. I helped him file the complaint against Bandy, but no tanks were found. In fact, Frank told me this morning he'd located the tanks in his boat."

"This morning?" Tony stared, poker-faced, at him.

"Yeah. On the phone."

"Where was he calling from?"

Jack squirmed, then shrugged. "He didn't say. I assumed from home, but maybe he was at work. I didn't ask."

"This complaint, you said nobody ever found anything. If that's the case, then why didn't the officer in charge sign off?" Tony tapped his finger on the complaint paper.

"I guess I forgot. I'm mostly involved in diving when I'm not handing out tickets. Complaints are a little out of my line."

"You were the officer in charge?" Tony's neck veins surfaced on reddened skin.

"Yeah, why not?"

"Damn it! Ellison. This was a family matter, and you forgot to sign the damn thing. I'd call that sloppy detective work. Plus, nothing—I repeat, nothing—on this job is out of your line! Is that clear?"

Ellison nodded and mumbled something like, "Yeah, sure."

"Whenever there's a family matter in the future, you call in somebody else. Is that clear?"

Jack's head bounced up and down; his face flushed, he rose and left the room.

Tony stared at the chair long after Jack disappeared down the hall. His clenched jaws pumped his neck veins full of blood. "What did you say about him, about the time he dived with you?" Tony asked.

"He raised a sand barrier, then swam into a cave. It was careless, not to mention, life threatening."

"Well, maybe I need to review Mr. Ellison's performance." He made a note on a pad, then turned to me. "Luanne, something isn't right here. We're investigating Angel's Bay Seafood. I need you and Vernon Drake to do something for me."

I was happy he didn't say Harry MacAllister, but then I realized one of us had to be a genuine deputy sheriff. Tony had enough confidence in me to let me hear conversations he had with Loman and his other men. I knew I was, in the eyes of the law, an acting agent of the department, but Tony had always gone to MacAllister for this kind of help before. I was second choice, but he wasn't reminding me of that now.

CHAPTER SEVENTEEN

Vernon drove the interstate over the speed limit. "We're meeting an agent in Pensacola," he said.

"FBI?"

"DEA."

"Drugs? Is that what this is all about?"

"We got an alert from the DEA that a steady supply of cocaine is coming into the north Florida area from an unknown source. Then, Amado and his detectives found stepped-up activity in the Gulf with Angel's Bay Company. He wants us to surveil their boats off the coast. That's all."

"That's all? Just go out into the Gulf, watch for drug smugglers, then report back to Sir Amado?" I aimed the air-conditioning vent toward the ceiling.

Vernon turned to me and grinned mischievously. "Yeah," he said, "not asking too much, right?"

The high foliage of giant oaks on top of rolling red clay hills gave way to flatlands with pines and palmettos, a sign that we were nearing saltwater. After pulling off the interstate, Vernon drove down a highway lined with marshy ditches. White egrets poked about the reeds for small fish. The road ended at a dock. The main pier where all the legitimate fishing boats tied up, after a long day on saltwater, was nearly a half mile down the bay. Three boats sat moored to a metal pier. Two were clearly marked as US government vehicles. The other, a plain speedboat outfitted with fishing gear, could have belonged to any local fisherman.

"Evrett Henderson." A compact, balding man in neatly pressed dark-blue pants, beige jacket and red tie held a badge for Vernon, who showed his in return. The DEA agent's eyes darted nervously around as he spoke, but when Vernon talked to him, the agent focused robot-like on his eyes.

"You plan on going out in a boat dressed like that?" Vernon said as he eyed the standard dress of any agent for any aspect of government. His own jeans, tee shirt, wind jacket, and dark glasses matched my attire. Both of us wore bathing suits under our clothing.

"I had to meet with some people before you came. Can't shatter the image, right?" He smiled slightly, then entered one of the large government boats. When he appeared again, he was dressed for life on the Gulf: white tee shirt, jeans, boat shoes, and a captain's hat. The perfect tourist.

After a briefing that included a warning to stay inconspicuous, Henderson led us to the fishing gear we would use, our guise to watch one of the Angel's Bay Seafood fishing vessels. Beneath the rods, reels, nets, and bait tank, lay a stash of field glasses and ammunition. I assumed Vernon and Evrett had the guns. We would be outside the limits of the law, instructed only to watch, not act. The Coast Guard had been alerted to our mission, but they would not follow us. Any radio contact would have to be for emergency only as the fishing vessel might be able to listen to communication.

"Amado tell you to bring any gear?" Henderson grabbed my elbow.

"We didn't bring diving equipment," I said.

"Good! The last thing I need are two frogmen playing heroics in the middle of the ocean. Just remember, we're in deep water, okay?" He squeezed my elbow.

Vernon whispered to me as we followed Henderson to the unmarked speed boat. "He means don't get him in deep shit!"

Since there hadn't been a storm on the Gulf this summer, the water would be clear. Even if we didn't catch any fish, we'd surely see them swimming around the boat. I tied on a large straw bonnet as we headed into the ceaseless sunlight. Vernon shoved an old fishing hat on his bald pate, and Henderson pulled a faded Florida State University shirt over his bare arms and replaced his captain's hat with a cap. He piloted the boat for miles, waving to other fishermen on the way. They could have been locals, or other agents sent to watch us.

When we finally came within sight of a fishing boat, I realized just how powerful our little motor was. The government wasted nothing on cheap models. Henderson slowed, allowing the engine to idle. He took a pair of glasses, and gazed off into the distance. Within a few minutes, he nodded toward the cache of equipment, where we found more field glasses.

Placing the glasses to my eyes, I could see Angel's Bay Seafood painted underneath *Athene* on the side of a rusting ship, badly in need of scraping and repainting. "Wonder if they've got the Goddess of Wisdom on board."

"What?" Henderson asked.

"Nothing," I said. "What now?"

"We fish and we watch. If you catch anything, haul it in. Don't get caught tossing the fish back. These people sometimes send divers into the water to unsnarl a net or something. That's what you're here for according to Amado. You're the experts on diving. If you see anything atypical of a diver, speak up."

"Like what?" I asked.

"I don't know. I'm not a diver. But like I said, if somebody watched us catching fish, then tossing them back in the ocean, don't you think they'd suspect us of being up to something else?"

We nodded, somewhat perplexed about what we could possibly see from surface side.

"It's going to be a long, hot afternoon." Henderson untangled the gear.

I leaned back on the vinyl seat. Vernon handed me a rod and reel with some fish bait on the hook. I hoped nothing would bite. In spite of my days in the water, I hated fishing, cringed when the squirmy things came out of the water. If you captured them, had them under your control, they struggled for life, and I just couldn't stand that.

"We'll take turns with the glasses, but somebody should be looking at all times," said Henderson.

"The stakeout in the middle of the Gulf of Mexico," Vernon laughed as he cast his line overboard.

Being the one with the big hat, I spent more time with the glasses. From a distance, it would be difficult to tell what I was doing in the shadows of that brim.

The day dragged, the sun glowed molten lead, and the backs of our shirts dripped with sweat. We soaked our arms in sunblock, drank soda from a cooler, and ate ham sandwiches—their saltiness drying our mouths. Henderson said the salt in the ham was good for our sweating and possible dehydration. When we couldn't stand sodas anymore, we went to bottled water.

"I'm going for a dip," said Vernon, suddenly removing his jeans and shirt. Before I could say anything, he slipped over the side, swam around a few minutes, then hauled back into the boat.

"Had to take a leak," Henderson said calmly. "Just say when

you need to go. If we were only men, we wouldn't bother to jump over the side."

I nearly burst into laughter, but Henderson didn't seem amused. He didn't seem anything. He had done too many of these stakeouts; he'd become jaded.

I picked up the glasses again, and from my shady brim, I watched two divers go over the side of the *Athene*. They stayed on the surface for a moment, signaling something to those on deck, then disappeared. They stayed under so long that I was about to put down the glasses and take another sip of water. That's when I saw two swimmers pushing a flat raft from the other side of the ship. It had heavy floats on two sides. The swimmers wore flippers, but no tanks. When they stationed the raft near the spot where the divers had been, they climbed on top and sat, doing nothing. Guessing they were waiting for something, I kept the glasses focused.

Within minutes, two divers surfaced on one side of the raft. The two men on board pulled up the divers' tanks and masks while the men in the water, lighter without the heavy cylinders, climbed on board. The raft seemed crowded, but all four men pulled small oars from the sides of the raft and rowed back around the ship.

"Could be some easy way they've found to get everything back on board," Vernon said as the raft disappeared. "I've never seen anything like it before."

"What color were the first two wetsuits?" I asked as I watched two more men go off the side of the ship, again in full diving gear.

"Black and yellow," said Vernon. "Lots of diving companies use wetsuits like uniforms."

"Well, these are red and black." The two divers hit the water, made the same waving motion, then disappeared into the depths.

Henderson picked up his glasses. At the same moment his fishing line jerked. "Damn! Somebody help me get this bastard up."

Vernon leaned over and the two of them pulled up a large grouper, his tail fanning the air in desperation. I pushed as far away from the squirming fish as I could, until Henderson tucked it into the ice chest.

"Who gets to eat him?" asked Vernon.

"I do, damn it!" Henderson shook ice off his hands. The screaming Seminole face on his shirt reminded me of the silent scream that grouper must be making about now.

I returned my attention to the ship. The wait was interminable. We soaked down in more sunblock, and all three of us did what I called the urinary dive over the side. The water was warm on the surface, cool at the chest, and even cooler below the waist, a refreshing change from the incessant sun light. I felt like I was peeing in somebody's pool and he knew it. Both men turned their heads, but it was still like being in a bathroom that had no door.

"The raft is coming back," Vernon said as I slid into the boat. I grabbed my glasses, dripping salt water over the seat.

"They're loading their equipment..." I stopped because, again, they seemed too crowded. Two men on the raft, two men in the water, their tanks.... "Hey! These guys are going down with one tank on their backs and coming back with two!"

"Shit!" Henderson grabbed his glasses.

"You're right. They're unloading onto the raft. Nothing else but an extra tank each." Vernon nodded to Evrett.

"That's it, I'll betcha! Hauling in dope inside those tanks." Henderson started pulling in the fishing lines. "Anybody need a last leak? It's going to take a while to get back to shore."

"Can't you radio any of this now?" I asked as he fumbled with the starter.

"Too easy to hear over radios. Besides we don't know for sure there's anything in those tanks. Although I'm willing to bet all the grouper in the Gulf there is." The engine gave a thrust on the first punch of the starter button. We turned around, making a circular wake and headed for Pensacola.

Vernon and I sat in the outer office of the local DEA headquarters while Henderson briefed his bosses and some people from the Coast Guard. By the time he came back to us, we were weary with sunburn and hunger.

"Okay, guys. Coast Guard is taking over for now. Tell Amado what we saw, then wait. You want to find a place to eat?" Henderson rubbed his head. "Damn hats make me itch."

"Thought we might eat that grouper raw if you didn't come out soon," said Vernon. "We might find a place on the way back to Tallahassee."

Henderson forgot about us and his hunger when he realized the grouper was still in the boat. He waved us off and scurried to the dock.

"There's a great place to eat down the coast. Has Southern fish if you want it, but also grills on mesquite wood and serves sourdough bread. You interested?" Vernon's entire face smiled, his eyes twinkling more than just an invitation to dinner.

The Frisco Wharf didn't only serve food, it served beds in the form of an attached motel. Vacation vans and overloaded station wagons lined the parking area. A Vacancy sign tried hard to flash in the sunset.

Inside, a steady breeze blew from air-conditioning vents, cooling my skin that reeked of coconut-scented lotion.

"Nothing could be so perfect," I said. I watched from the restaurant window as the sun eased slowly into the ocean. A few pines and a palm tree turned black in the background glow, the water taking on a sparkle from an algae that reminded me of stars on a Christmas tree. Not many customers had come in from fishing yet, leaving us a quiet broken occasionally by a waiter pouring water into a crystal glass.

Vernon leaned toward me with his own water glass. "There's a vacancy."

"I know. I saw it as soon as we drove in. If you wait long enough, somebody will take it."

"Touche!" He stood up, went out the door, and returned in less than twenty minutes. I was nibbling on a broiled shrimp when he sat down. "Number sixteen, the farthest from the office." He dropped the key on the table and picked up his fork.

We relaxed our tired bodies with soft, firm, mutual massages, gripping and caressing skin and muscle until the nerves tingled with anesthetic, numbing the fatigue and filling the joints with morphins. Once again alert, we explored, guiding each other into territories no one else could. It was a night of total giving over to curiosity, of throwing inhibitions to the sea breeze. Neither desired to wander into the realm of hurt, so our meanderings were gentle, determined, but embracing the soul along with the body. Following deep currents, we let the moment drown us together. When sleep finally overtook us, we drifted off to the gentle beat of rain on palmetto bushes outside the window.

As we ate scrambled eggs in a mom-and-pop cafe some-where outside Ft. Walton, I asked, "Don't you think we should call Amado?"

"I did. Last night when you were taking a shower. You don't think I wanted business hanging over my head, did you?"

My face grew hot. Vernon smiled at me from across the table; his tanned dimples seemed to go straight into his ears. I thought it something close to precious the way the skin on his bald head, just at the top of his brow, crinkled slightly every time he did his wide grin. I fantasized discovering more details about him, even more than the ones I found last night.

"What's the next step?" I said, trying to regain composure.

"He's had contact with Henderson. The DEA is working with the Coast Guard to find out if the seafood company has any contact on the other side—meaning the Mexican side of the Gulf. Our job is finished with the Pensacola scene for now. I imagine we'll be looking into the company's business around Tallahas-see."

We drove leisurely back to Florida's capital, approaching from the south side where lowlands eased into the red clay hills once again. We drove up the slope in front of the old capitol building, passing through a refurbished street that had once been full of stores that sold cow feed in jute sacks, then headed north past colonial homes and new steel office buildings nested among moss-draped oaks as old as the state itself.

We pulled into the Sheriff's Department lot. My Honda sat under a shady oak, where I had left it. Vernon typed his report, which I countersigned. Then I drove myself home.

Bailey Construction had completed most of the roof repair on one side. They would soon have to remove the tin from the other side and replace it with shingles. The workers told me Zull

161

was out of the hospital, but would take a day to recuperate, that is, if he didn't get so mad he'd go hunting for Bandy. As for Joe, no one had found him.

I spent the afternoon cleaning, then preparing a dinner of roast pork and potatoes for Vernon. I just didn't care at the moment who killed two women and hid their bodies in the springs. I didn't even care that Harry MacAllister had returned, and I only slightly noticed when I heard the putt-putt of a motor move down the river.

The night proved no less sensuous than the one before, although with more grace and less abandonment. We fell asleep in each other's arms, again to the rhythmic beat of light rain on vegetation.

Sometime in the night I woke, and in my haze thought I again heard the putt-putt, thought it had shut down outside, but the rain had begun to pound. I fell asleep again with my arms and legs curled around Vernon's strong back. He grunted and put one arm over my leg.

The next morning, Vernon shouted through the shower, "Amado's got a man out front. He wants me downtown right now."

I shut off the water to hear Vernon talking. "What's the deal with the divers? You got enough?"

"What's going on?" I asked as I swiped a towel over my body and stepped into the hall.

"A drowning at Lake Tompkin." Vernon hurried into his jeans. "Kids can't stay away from the dam. Two are at the bottom for sure. Another can't be accounted for. Amado's called all of us in. I'll see you later."

I nodded, kissed him goodbye, and returned to the bathroom. I wanted a lazy day, one with my house and my swamp. I had come here for peace, but I was getting more excitement than I could stand.

Later, while I sat on the front porch in a position where the sun would shine on my hair, drying it, I heard a car pull up. I wanted it to be Vernon, returning to tell me the kids had been rescued after all. Instead, Harry MacAllister stood outside the porch screen, his face smiling like a guilty alley cat.

Without asking, he opened the door and sat in a rocker. "I've got a new grant, Luanne, to explore some of the larger sinks around here. I've always wanted to map them, to find out where the water begins. I'll need some volunteers who can dive. You game? I can get the linguistics department to release you for another year."

Harry tempted me with freedom. I didn't want to be around him, but his offer would give me another year in my swamp, another year of not answering to deans and curriculum committees. Could I answer to Harry MacAllister?

CHAPTER EIGHTEEN

Harry insisted on taking a swim off my landing. I fumed a while, then drove to the paved road to call Vernon about the children. He sounded awful, like he wanted to drown himself. I wanted him here, but he claimed the perpetual paperwork had to be done immediately. "The kids didn't make it," he said. Then, in a choking voice, he said a soft "bye" with no promise of a visit to my swamp for the evening.

I returned to brood on my porch, rocking and thinking about finding drowned children. Harry appeared from the trees across the road. He brushed a towel through his thick hair, but let his wet body drip water into a puddle atop mushy leaves.

"Do you know somebody is using the bank out there, the place just above that cave?" He wrapped the towel around his neck.

"And do you know you shouldn't be standing in this swamp barefooted?"

"Yeah?" he said, mocking a terrified face. "Who's been coming by here in a boat?"

The motor boat, its putt-putt going up and down the river at twilight, and in the middle of the night, flashed into my head.

"You don't suppose..." I sat up straight.

"What?"

"There's another body in a cave?" I couldn't believe we'd find another one, and just outside my door. I dashed for my diving equipment. As soon as Harry saw what I was doing, he ran to his Volkswagen. With no back seat, it had enough room to stow his tank. We dragged our cylinders and flippers through wet pine needles and decaying oak stems to the landing. Neither said a word until we geared up.

"You lead?" Harry asked.

"Of course." I went into the water feet first.

I swam near the top until right before the cave. Surfacing briefly, I glimpsed the muddy spot on the bank where someone had dragged something heavy. Turning tail up, I dived into the depths, pushing myself through the clear water, feeling its cold currents against my face mask and their residual force touching the tips of my flippers. The cave opening was blocked. Metallic, rounded pieces about the diameter of a bowling ball, flat from my view, prevented an arm from reaching inside. They had length, too, and when Harry swam beside me, we pushed the things around until we realized they were diving cylinders, old ones, rusted in places. I tried pulling one out, but they were secured tightly. Harry stuck his fingers between one cylinder and the cave wall and pulled out a heavy chain, a padlock holding it together. Whoever had secured them here had found a place to attach them that wouldn't let go. I motioned to Harry to surface.

"We'd better call Amado," I said after we reached the dock. Harry nodded and pointed an "after you" to the makeshift ladder.

We pulled on clothes over our suits and piled into Harry's VW. It bumped like a carnival car all the way to the hotel at Palmetto Springs.

"You got to get yourself wired," said Harry. He gripped the gear shift with his right hand. "You're too involved in nasty business to stay out here with no communication."

When I called Tony, he stayed silent for too long. The events with the kids had taken its toll on the entire department. "Our divers have had it for today. After this ordeal in Lake Tompkin, I can't send them under again," he said. After a pause, he went on. "I will send some stakeouts. They'll have to sit in the swamp, but they've done worse." He paused again. "Luanne... do you think I could sleep over?"

Tony on my living room sofa! I almost hoped the raccoons would do their number again.

After speaking to Tony, Harry dropped me off then sped away in his Volkswagen. I thought I'd seen the last of him for the day. Just as well. I was growing too comfortable with his presence, and I didn't like it.

Around seven o'clock, a marked patrol car pulled up. Harry got out first and looked at me with a "forgive me" expression.

"Tony wants me here. Can you put me up, too? I'll take the floor in a sleeping bag."

"Hope you don't mind," mumbled Tony as he peeked under the steps.

I minded like hell! Not only was Tony slipping my former lover and deserter into my privacy, he was also giving him my spot in this case. Resentment washed over me, but I swallowed it. "Okay." I stood in my half-done living room, fuming one moment, chastising myself for being childish the next.

I plopped into a porch rocker just as another patrol car pulled up and deposited two more men at my steps. They piled sleeping bags and radio equipment on my porch. Then, both patrol cars backed down the dirt road, their speed kicking up forest floor debris that danced in the sunlight.

"We don't want a visible presence around here," said Tony.

I heard the two men tell him some deputies had taken up spots in the swamp, literally on the swamp floor. Harry busied himself with Amado's directions, moving the gear into the living room. Both avoided looking at me.

I left them to their plans and slipped upstairs. Taking a position in a small room full of boxes and Daddy's old chair, I could see most of the river directly in front of the house. I scanned the jutting bank with field glasses. Rain clouds blocked the light in spite of a full moon. I felt for those men, lying on their stomachs in the damp swamp grass, fighting off bugs, and God knows what else.

Time moved in slow motion. I could hear Tony and Harry saying something to each other, but most of the night was quiet. The rain threatened, but never really happened, outside of a slow drizzle for a half hour. I dozed in a wicker chair, my neck aching each time I jerked awake. I would peer through the glasses, and seeing nothing, allow myself to nod off again. The last time, I must have drifted into deep sleep.

Suddenly, two male voices sounded from below, one urgently ordering, "Go! Go!"

I grabbed the glasses to see one person climbing into a small boat crowded with cargo, the outline of another person at the motor. Assuming someone had gone into the cave to get the tanks, I ran downstairs and joined Tony and Harry on the path to the river.

"You two stay out of range!" Tony shouted at us as he pulled his gun. At the same time, two speedboats surrounded an old motorboat. Two deputies on the jutted bank burst out of the bushes and held guns on the two surprised men. They sat squeezed between rusty scuba cylinders.

"Place your hands in the air, then come out of the boat

when the deputies order you to!" shouted Tony. The men in the boat snapped their heads in his direction.

Chatter went back and forth over walkie-talkies, then a deputy on the jut tossed a rope. They pulled the boat closer, and ordered the men out of their vessel. On shore, the deputies pushed them to the ground, searched, and cuffed them. After that, my swamp lit up like a holiday lights festival with police vehicles, crime scene people, and three divers. Vernon was among them, but not Jack Ellison. By morning, DEA agents had joined the sheriff's department, and I—the diving authority on caves in these parts—served coffee on my front porch.

Vernon and his diving mates searched the cave area for more tanks, but the two arrested men had removed all of them. When he finished, he joined me on the porch, along with Harry and some uniformed men. I felt uneasy in the presence of the two men who had shared my intimacies. No one noticed, because the air sizzled with the excitement of the arrest. Cop adrenalin snapped from one bravado conversation to another. I drank in silence until Loman came in, his droopy lids belying his quick stride.

"We got the bastards, and the DEA got them on the other end!" He lifted his coffee cup in a toast. A basso cheer went up.

He told his story of the DEA, Henderson in particular, watching fishing boats on the Gulf. When Angel's Bay Seafood pulled into dock, the DEA went on board and found their evidence—four dummy diving cylinders full of cocaine. They had cleverly cut off the top part of the tanks, slipped in the packages of coke, then refitted the parts together, making them watertight.

"Their dealers in Mexico and South America were placing the stuff in those tanks—conveniently attaching them to a deep-

168

water wreck—then the guys on this side of the border picked them up at the same time they fished for daily market supplies. Agents are at the seafood company right now. One of the guys we arrested 'fessed up, said old Petroulious was the head of the local operation. We're getting a warrant to search The Greek Oyster, too."

"So what were these tanks doing here in this spring?" asked a deputy whose belly struggled against his tight belt. He pulled out a cellophane-wrapped sandwich and swallowed it in quarters.

"Probably one of their hiding places until the stuff could be put on the street." Loman beamed like the good boy at school.

"Who did you arrest?" I pointed in the direction of my landing.

"Two guys who worked for the seafood company, one of them a diver."

"Frank Ellison?"

Loman nodded, then the hoods over his eyes lifted for a second. "Damn! He's Jack's brother!" He slammed down his coffee cup so hard liquid splashed onto the floor, then he took off running toward the landing.

Officers in uniform, detectives in plainclothes, and stakeout men in fatigues stood amid the crime scene techs. They journeyed to the porch for something to drink, but never got far from their prisoners. Frank Ellison and his accomplice sat on the damp grass for over an hour. Finally, two deputies helped them up and guided them to a police car. They waited another hour before being carted off to the sheriff's lock-up. They probably sat in a holding cell for even more hours. The "boys" on the force called it the "think about it and weep" torture.

Amado, his eyes puffy from lack of sleep, came to the porch with Loman. "Luanne, I want you to guide Loman and the other officers to Frank's place. Take them to the barn with the tanks first. Just stay out of the way while they search. I'm going to the seafood company with some agents. We'll keep the rest of the officers here, on your porch if you don't mind?"

Loman spoke briefly to an officer who handed him the folded search warrant. I gave directions for making more coffee to a young cop, then joined Loman and two other men in an unmarked car. A patrol car followed us into the rising sun.

The same man in overalls stood in Ellison's front yard. He spoke directly to me, his eyes wide and frightened above grizzly whiskers. "Mr. Ellison said not to let you folks in the barn anymore, that he was done with that complaint. He was right mad about the last time I let you in, nearly fired me."

I shrugged and looked at Loman.

"Don't matter what Mr. Ellison said, sir. The court has given us a search warrant." He pulled out the folded paper and handed it to the man.

"I don't read so good." The man didn't unfold the paper. His hands trembled like a morning drinker.

"Don't matter. Just let us place it somewhere in the house. It says we can search the entire farm, including all structures and machinery on it. You got keys?" Loman stood in front of the man, his hand held out.

The man nodded, shrugged, and started toward the main house. Two men followed him inside. Loman and I waited until he returned with his keys jangling in his hands.

"That one," I pointed to the second barn, and the man took

us past the first one to the smaller structure, two detectives in tow.

There were only three tanks lined against the wall today. Each had the pencil line drawn around the top, the cutting line. "You need to look for the equipment that can cut these," I said as I pointed to the machinery, "then something like welding torches that could put on brackets or maybe grind the tops into a snug fit. I'll bet there are finished tanks around here someplace."

I found a torn wicker chair and moved it under a tree. From my position, I could hear the officers' remarks as well as see them through the double doors. I fidgeted during the long day, sitting then pacing under the oaks. I hated being on the sidelines. The old man in overalls stood with me sometimes, his head shaking in disbelief. I wanted to ask if he was completely in the dark about this operation, but I dared not talk to him about the case. Finally, a deputy faced him, and he made a statement.

"I been hired here for nearly six years, to do the grounds and sort of be caretaker. Ellison was good to me. He just said stay away from the equipment 'cause it could be dangerous. I thought that meant if I didn't know how to use it, I could cut myself. He had lots of people out here from time to time, mostly from that seafood company, but then he had his brother, too. His brother mostly visited inside the main house. Once in a while there were people I didn't know down to the barns, but they seemed okay to me. Didn't have women out here much, 'cept that gal that worked with him. She was all over him, and I don't think he liked it much. Always pushing her off him. Don't know her name, but she worked at the seafood company."

"Angie Stephoulous! I'll bet." I marched over to Loman. "Something was going on between those two. I'm sure of it. When she found out, or saw something, he whacked her!"

"Whacked?" Loman's droopy eyes twinkled. "Well, just maybe I've got a photo of the girl. Maybe this man can identify her." He pulled the photo from an envelope in his coat pocket and gave me a wink.

The man jabbed the picture with his gnarled finger. "That's the one! All over him, all the time!"

By evening, the evidence wagon was full. There were finished tanks, but most were in the process of being outfitted for drugs. There was machinery that cut, ground, and welded, and maps, ocean maps that pilots can read. Ellison had the perfect set up to camouflage this operation. He was a gentleman farmer, hiring others to raise corn and a few chickens while he worked in town. Even his caretaker was "just a good old boy" who didn't have the sense to smell for crime.

Loman had one of the patrol cars take me home. When I arrived, the young officer greeted me on my porch, his face weary with nothing to do but make coffee and guard an area that had been full of cops all day.

"Some construction guys came by," he said, "but we had to tell them the area was sealed off. Man said to call him." He handed me a dirty scrap of paper with Zull's name and phone number. I guessed he was back on the job now.

"Some other guy, a scrawny little fellow with a jumpy face, showed up at the end of the road, but he took off when he saw the cars. I got an officer to try and follow him, but he lost him. A friend of yours?"

I shook my head. "Likely somebody who was curious. We may be in the middle of the swamp, but I'll bet everybody in Fogarty Spring knows something's happened here." An icy feeling inside told me that jumpy face belonged to Joe Bandy.

That night, my last thought as I drifted into sleep was of

Pasquin. He was usually in the middle of things, wanting to know what went on, then exaggerating it to his cronies. I planned to check on him first thing in the morning.

The deputy they left to guard the place had either paced the boards or snored intermittently all night. Even the sounds of swamp insects dimmed with the competition. Finally, another officer showed up early and placed himself on my porch.

I dragged out of bed and met the new man who smiled and handed me a newspaper. He carried a large box of donuts under the other arm.

"Paper's alive this morning, ma'am!"

The headlines screamed of the local seafood market being the alleged headquarters for an international cocaine smuggling operation. All the arrested were named, including Frank Ellison and Arno Petroulious. DEA agents had taken most of the others off the boat in Pensacola. Toward the bottom of the article, the reporter added: *It is not known if the bodies found in caves in Palmetto Springs had any connection with the smuggling. However, one source said it's possible. Angelina Stephoulous was an employee of that firm.*

"Damn right, it was connected," I said under my breath.

"In my day, young ladies wouldn't dare use such language."

I turned around and laughed. "Pasquin! I planned to check on you this morning. Where have you been?"

"You got me into this, m'lady. I spent all day yesterday hosting lawmen who traveled down the river to the hunt camp, then searched up and down the river. They knew I'd been to the camp, was there the day they found Delia. When they got through asking me questions, they set up shop in my living room. Moved all my furniture back so they could navigate through the place. Won't

173

never be the same!"

I laughed. Finally someone made some space in that living room. I held the screen door for Pasquin as he steadied himself on the banister with one hand, his straw hat in the other. He made a gesture of looking between the steps as he came in.

"Old snake must have been frightened off by all these people, or did one of these lawmen shoot his head off?"

"No dead animals, yet. I suspect he's hiding far under the house or way back in the swamp."

"Long's it ain't under my foot." He sat in a rocker and immediately began fanning himself. The young cop eyed him suspiciously at first, then offered him coffee.

"Not unless it's my own brew, son. This stuff got way too much water in it. Lemonade or tea would be nice, Miss Luanne." He smiled in my direction, reminding me of the duties of a Southern hostess. If he had been younger and I less respectful of my elders, I would have told him where he could grow the lemons, but I frowned instead and headed for the kitchen.

I was stirring in the sugar when a silver truck pulled out of the trees onto the rutted road. Two men with all kinds of tools hanging from their belts got out and met my young officer on the path. By the time I got the lemonade to the front porch, the two men were standing at the bottom of the stairs.

"Ma'am, you asked for telephone lines out here. We got the poles up on the road, and we're here to wire your house. We need to come inside."

The officer held the screen door for them. They nodded to Pasquin who poured fresh liquid into a tall glass. "You fellows like some lemonade?"

I smiled. Fresh lemonade and a real phone all in one morning. Made me wonder what else could happen before sunset.

CHAPTER NINETEEN

With the owner of Bailey Construction Company under suspicion for drug smuggling, Zull took a few of the workers and formed his own loose unit. Some of the same men who worked at the hunt camp came out for two weeks to roof the other side of my house and to refurbish the upstairs rooms. My swamp dwelling took on the demeanor of a forest cabin—one step up in the class category.

"You want this put somewhere special?" Zull said. He breathed hard at the top of the stairs. He had carried my mother's old trunk from the extra room.

"In my bedroom. I guess I need to take another look through it."

My mother regarded this trunk as her private cache, and we respected that. After Daddy died, I had all his household things transported to me. Until now, I felt like a marauder sacking the ruins, and I stayed away from nosing around it too often.

While hammers and drills pounded in the large room down the hall, I sat on the floor and pushed back the trunk lid. The odor hit me like opening a sealed pyramid, the oldness escaping with an almost discernible gasp. I put aside the photos I had seen so many times, then rifled the papers sitting in the top section, afraid to look at them. Tears would come for good old times, maybe open wounds in the process. I took the first paper.

It was my diploma, my bachelor's degree in English. Beneath it, pictures of my graduation—BA, MA, then PhD. Why did I go through a ceremony for all three? I laughed at myself, so proud in my robes, each time adding a sash. Getting those degrees and becoming a professor had been important to me. I wondered if Daddy was proud, too. He had no pictures of weddings or births, no grandchildren. It hit me then. My father never had a grandchild. Why do I realize this now? I dug further. More papers, including my mother's death certificate—so young.

I don't remember exactly what she looked like, but I see her in this picture. Pretty. She must have been very kind. Daddy married her after all, and then didn't seek out another wife after she was gone. But don't happily married people usually want to marry again when the spouse dies?

I had heard that somewhere, but I squelched the idea. My father adored my mother. It was that simple in my mind, my child's mind that surfaced when I dealt with my parents. I pulled up the top tray. Underneath, there were large albums, crumbling from age. Flipping through several pictures of women in flapper-type dresses, men in knee pants, then women in high collars and long skirts, I rifled through a treasure house of family history. Photos of this house, brand-new and white, in a cleared-out area. No one would have recognized it, the one with sagging brown boards in a jungle cocoon.

There were some more modern photos, modern around the fifties. One I remembered that my father often showed me in the days after Mother died. There he was in his army uniform with a couple of medals from the Korean war, standing behind my mother in her tailored suit, a flat hat covering her pulled-back hair with Mamie Eisenhower bangs in the front. Their smiles were genuine, happy to be together on the porch of this house.

Another photo reminded me of someone. My mother sat in a rocker, a handsome man beside her. She poured, perhaps, lemonade into his glass. Both were smiling, but he looked straight at her, not into the camera nor at the glass. I turned on the back and read. *Eleanor and Dorian, summertime.* Pasquin! He lived and worked on the river, a thriving economy back then. He looked frightfully handsome, and his smile betrayed an interest in this lovely young woman. I wasn't born yet. Pasquin would have been close to forty. Never married, but had lots of ladies. I replaced the photo in the album. Grasping an envelope the size to mail large things in, I felt like a grave robber. The glue on the flap gave way easily, sounding like dry leaves underfoot in an ancient cemetery. Lined paper, the kind kids bought to put in their school notebooks, rested inside. Each had a date at the top, from December '54 backward to December '53.

I felt like a voyeur, as the diary's intimate vocabulary flashed before my eyes. *Marvelous! Charming! Virile! Fogy, forgive me!* Daddy told me she called him Fogy.

My mother had a crush—I dared not say an affair—that lasted one year! It had to be Dorian Pasquin, but his name never actually appeared. Maybe she imagined a lover, created someone to temporarily replace my father.

I slammed the trunk lid shut. Zull came to the bedroom door, hammer in hand, and asked if something was wrong. I feigned my annoyance, saying the lid had slipped. I had to get out, to breathe. I sought refuge in the swamp.

A light rain fell, but if I walked among the trees, I wouldn't get wet. I kicked aside any debris that sat on the path, even created new paths to the river only to find deep muddy spots that would have taken me up to my knees. Without realizing it, I wound around the swamp and ended up downriver. A few feet ahead, I could see the shabby vacation cabin that belonged to a family who lived in Alabama. They traveled in a motorhome, but when they came here to fish, they left the vehicle in a Fogarty Spring lot and used their boat to take them up and down the river.

I moved into the heavy reeds and marshy soil to take a peek at the old place. Its boards were almost as saggy as mine, but the windows looked new, and an outside air conditioner stood on a cement slab. The motor was silent; the people weren't here. Their deck overlooked the river, a short stairway leading down to their dock. The area over the water had recently been repaired. The front door, opposite this side, faced a small foot path that led directly outward to the forest. There was no porch. This family's whole reason for being here was the river, not the swamp.

Avoiding some clumps of muddy grass, I found another short set of steps leading up to the deck from the mushy swamp floor. It must not have been used much. Vegetation curled around the rotting boards. Moving carefully, I stood on the first step. When I leaned over to find the next mud-covered step, my eye caught something underneath the deck.

The water was shallow and muddy, but deep enough to float a small boat on. A rowboat, its oars resting under the narrow seat slats, swayed gently in a soft wake. It looked homemade and not recently painted, but seaworthy all the same. I backed away and went to the front where I could see through a window if I stood on my tiptoes. Even then, I had to peer through the narrow gap in some green curtains. A stove and a plastic trash can sat within my view. A brown grocery sack with the market's logo sat atop the stove. I could see nothing else, but if I had to make a guess, I'd say someone was staying here. A friend of the Alabama family? Maybe a member of their family? An intruder? It gave me something to think about besides my unfaithful mother and my friend—was he?—Pasquin.

I walked home, avoiding Pasquin's well-formed path, and trucked through muddy water, dodging soil-colored frogs that looked like rocks suddenly coming to life. When I reached my porch, a familiar face welcomed me.

"Haven't seen you in a while, Luanne." Vernon's grin, still sending thrills up my neck, seemed hesitant. He held the screen open for me and gave me the bear hug I needed.

"Tony said you were on assignment or something."

"Yeah, well, we need to talk about that."

Power saws and automatic nail guns sounded above. I suggested we find a nice air-conditioned cafe. Vernon suggested his place.

We drove in silence except for a comment on the progress of the house. When Vernon reached over and took my hand, I relaxed. Maybe this was just his way.

The entrance to Vernon's land looked like his smile—broad, gaping, and friendly to the point of enticement. He had paved his driveway and planted dogwood trees on either side. We drove down a slight incline into a canopy of more dogwood trees, their leaves solid green in midsummer.

"Must be spectacular in springtime!" I said.

Newly-mowed lawn blanketed the ground throughout his planted forest. In spots, circular gardens of bright flowers stood out like precious gems. When we finally arrived in front of a small, natural-wood cabin, crepe myrtle bushes of red, purple, and pink engulfed the front wall.

"It's unbelievable! When do you find time to take care of all this?"

"Riding a lawn mower is great therapy." He winked at me,

179

but didn't smile.

Inside was masculine and basic. His few pictures were large, framed ocean scenes he said a friend painted for him. Off the living room, he had set up an office with shelves of books and his diving and promotion plaques on the wall. Behind this, his bedroom faced the back, a lake front. A wooden deck the width of the house led from his room to a narrow walk that finally ended at a square dock standing well into the lake. There was no boat in sight.

We sat on the deck, sipping soda and watching someone across the lake trying to water ski. Tension grew in our silence.

"You were going to talk to me about something?" I said it softly, almost sure it would be something to hurt me.

He took a long drink, then crushed the can in his hand. "I have this problem. When you hear about it, you may want out of this relationship, if we really have one."

"We have one." I stopped, surprised at myself for having admitted that. "Go on."

"Those kids in Lake Tompkin, they didn't make it."

I nodded. The tragedy was common knowledge by now.

"Tony called me in, because he needed me, but ordinarily he wouldn't in a case like that."

I looked at him, afraid to ask why. When he continued to speak, it was like a roller coaster he couldn't stop.

"When I was married the first time. I had a kid. Andy. Best little kid you've ever seen. We lived near the St. Marks River. His mother scolded me about letting him play at the edge. I thought he had to get used to it, to learn how to handle the river like I did. Got to form your kid just like yourself, right? One day he drifted down there when I wasn't around. His mother couldn't find him, and well, you can guess the rest." He paused, then added, "He was three-and-a-half-years-old."

"Vernon, I'm sorry, but you can't think I'd reject you because of a tragedy like that."

"It's not the tragedy. It's the way it's left me. I have a problem with alcohol. You must have noticed I don't drink. I'm okay until something like that Tompkin drowning happens, then I can't handle it. I've been known to go on a drunk for days. Amado has covered for me every time, but I don't know how long that's going to last."

"Have you tried to get help…"

"Yes! Damn it! And I am getting better, I guess." He hesitated for a moment. "When I got home that day, my wife and the cops were looking all over for Andy. I put on my gear and went into the river. Found him caught in a clump of river grass. He must have slipped in the shallows. You know how the river can slant downward suddenly. That's the kind of spot he waded in. I'll never forget the paleness of his face…" Vernon stopped and rubbed his eyes.

"What happened to your wife?"

"She went crazy for a while, then moved back with her parents in Jacksonville. Not too long after, she sent me divorce papers. But that was all right. We reminded each other of Andy too much. Never would have made it. She's remarried. Has a little girl now."

I have never been good at consoling people. Right from my mother's funeral, when I refused to believe she was a real person lying there, to Pasquin's cousin, I ached to see people crying over a coffin, but I didn't know how to make the pain go away. Whatever I said to Vernon, abandonment wasn't in the cards. I stood behind him, cradling his head. He held on to my hand, and we remained this way until the skier finally got up and made it all the

181

way across the lake.

I stayed with Vernon all night. His caresses were strong, enclosing me in embraces that seemed to make me part of him. Maybe this was his way of holding onto love that for him was forever fleeing.

On the way back to my house the next morning, I told Vernon about the river cabin and its boat. He seemed surprised, didn't think the department had checked out anything like that. They had turned their attention to the hunt camp area, looking for more drugs. At my door, he promised to give Tony the information, then pulled me to his chest. He drove away with the big grin plastered across his face again.

Zull and his men took advantage of the cooler morning air and were already pounding nails. He came downstairs and met me on the porch as I waved to Vernon.

"I need to ask you, ma'am. You ever have any trouble with Joe Bandy, other than the break-in and the day he bashed your windows?"

"Isn't that enough?"

"He's been spotted by some people over in Fogarty and some in Palmetto. One said he even saw him out by the paved road here."

I had a flash of the scraggly man who ran when he saw the force of cops in the woods, the day they arrested Ellison.

"Is he a danger to me?"

"He's a danger to everybody when he's high on something, which is just about all the time. He ain't none too happy with me, either. If you see anything like him around here, holler, okay?"

I agreed to scream a Tarzan warning.

"And, just in case, I'm packing lead." He lifted his sweat-soaked shirt. He wore a belt with a holster attachment on it, the

182

butt of a gun sticking out above his ample hip.

I spent the morning mapping out spots to put new furniture and going over paint colors. By lunch, I had redecorated all the upstairs without spending a penny. Preparing to make sandwiches for everyone, I heard Pasquin's familiar drawl on the porch.

"Sheriff wants me in to look at a picture. Wants you, too. You aiming to drive us?"

CHAPTER TWENTY

DELIA

"You asked me to get this to you some time ago. I guess I got busy and forgot, but now we need your help." Tony spread out several blow-ups of Carmina's body in the spring. Two enhanced the arm with the Bible tied around it. Pasquin squinted, pushing the picture back and forth. I'd never seen him wear glasses and I wondered now if he didn't need them. Tony came to his rescue with a magnifying glass.

"It looks like one of those Bibles I had in Sunday school as a child," I said as I tried to make sense of the fuzzy black square. "See, it even has a zipper. I had one like that once."

"But there's no writing, no Holy Bible printed on it anywhere." Tony leaned over me.

"It's probably on the other side," added Loman who had joined us with more blow-ups. "Here, these are larger."

"There's something not quite right with it," I said as I traced the visible zipper. "See, it's not exactly square, more of a rectangle, and the zipper starts at the top, goes around one longer side, across the narrow bottom and up again on the other long side. That would mean the Bible would open up; the top of the case would fold back above the words. I never had a Bible that did that. The cover always laid back with the pages, like a regular book cover does."

Pasquin ignored us. Suddenly, he slapped the photo on the table and placed the glass over it.

"That's where they went!" He looked up at us and grinned, his cheeks waking with wrinkles. "The silver dollars. I remember now. Carmina bought a zip case for hers."

"About how many would have been in there?" Tony asked.

"Hard to say. We've been collecting them for years. If she didn't sell any, maybe fifty—or more. Who's to know?"

Tony paced to the door, then turned back to us. "Even if it was a hundred, I don't think drug operators would waste time with them. They might steal them on the spot, but tie them to the woman's arm?"

We sat quietly. No one had a solution.

Tony continued. "Frank Ellison knows a lot, but he's not talking. Afraid of what the others will do to him. The only thing we've got so far is a fearful reaction when we mention Joe Bandy." He paced again, his forehead wrinkled.

"What about that boarder?" I asked.

"Rentell? His alibis checked out. Was nowhere near Tallahassee that night."

"But he was in the house lots of times, right? Didn't he say he had rooms all over the south?" I asked. "Why not look in those rooms to see if he hides silver dollars."

Tony and Loman shot a glance at each other. Pasquin took a deep breath, picked up his straw hat and slammed it back on the table. "Will you young cannons get the rust out and do as the lady says!"

Tony gave Loman orders to locate the addresses Rentell had told us about in Tifton. He walked with me to the car. Pasquin dragged behind, curious about the various offices and their stacks of files and evidence filling every available space. "Don't know how they sort one case from another around here," we heard him say to himself.

"Have you seen Vernon?" Tony asked without looking at me.

"Yes, and I know about his son. It puts him in a bad way every now and then."

"He'll be all right. He's better now than a few weeks ago. You won't regret sticking by him." Tony still didn't look at me. Instead, he nodded to a colleague coming into the hall from the reception room.

"What about Jack Ellison? Is he still with the sheriff's office?" I asked.

"Yep. On the desk right now, until we get his brother fully charged."

"What does that mean?"

"It means Frank won't talk. He knows a lot more than we found out about that operation, but he clams up. Scared of the operators behind this. And, I don't blame him. He talks, they shoot."

"Do you still think Joe Bandy had something to do with this?"

"Positive. And thanks for that tip about the cabin on the river. We've watched it before, but it looks like there may be some action around there now. Owners have given us permission to do what we have to do."

Pasquin and I rode in silence for a few miles, then he got the talking disease and wouldn't stop with how things were back then—back when he worked on the river and knew all the merchants along the banks.

"Loaded up tobacco and cotton at one end, delivered it at the other where it got loaded onto a freight train and sent to the factory. Logs, too. Pines in this part of the world were sold for furniture and paper mills. We'd float up and down that river, right over those spring caves, through alligators and all. A real wild river back then, yes sirree."

"Wilder than now?"

"Sure, 'cept where people had cleared out the bush and vines to build a house or maybe a big old warehouse. None of those left now—warehouses, I mean. Guess the jungle took over those areas, but it was sure hopping back then."

"What happened during the Korean war?"

"That's the time I'm telling you about. Best years of my life. Of course, I didn't have to go off to war. They needed me here, not to mention that I was a little overage." He chuckled to himself.

"My father went." I could feel my heart pounding. I wanted to scream at him, but I wasn't sure what I'd say.

"Yeah, he did. Fine thing, too. Got a couple of medals. Your mama was pretty proud when he came home. You wasn't around, yet, were you?"

I turned briefly to look at him. If he had been fooling around with my mother, wouldn't he know I wasn't even born yet?

"Nope. Guess I was an aftermath of all the fuss."

"Yes," said Pasquin and looked out the window. He suddenly went quiet.

"Pasquin, did you ever get close to my mother?"

He didn't look at me. "Meaning?"

"You know what I mean. My father was away for a time during the war. Did you and she—shall we say—comfort each other."

"I comforted her the best I could, Luanne. She took the comfort she wanted. Let it stay private, ma'am."

"When my father returned, did she need any more comfort?"

He looked out the window again. "Not from me."

I took a quick glance at my face in the rearview mirror: dark-brown hair, blue eyes, pale skin. I was tall, five feet eight. Pasquin was short for a man, olive skin, brown eyes, white hair that was probably jet black once. I shook my head; he couldn't be my father. I looked too much like Daddy. Taking a deep breath, I turned onto the paved road then dodged holes in the ruts until I reached home.

We stood outside the car. Just as Pasquin was about to say something to me, Zull came running onto the porch, hammer in hand.

"Hey! We spotted Bandy in the woods back there," he pointed to the back of the house. "We just called the sheriff! Mr. Pasquin, you better not go walking off through the swamp right now."

Pasquin and I went inside. All work stopped on the roof. Shouting sounded from one side of the house to the other, "You see anything?" "Some brush just moved over that way!"

"How do you know it was Bandy?" I asked Zull.

"Ma'am, I'd know that screwy dude from miles. He's wild, especially when he gets on the stuff, and from the way he was running, I'll bet he's on the stuff big time."

"Does he have a gun?"

"Didn't see any, but he's probably got a pistol under his shirt somewhere. Knife, too. He's never without a knife." Zull's eyes resembled a deer's caught in headlights. They belied his thick body that looked as though it could crush a whole field of Joe Bandy's. He was scared of this man, the little guy who had come at him with a bat, like a feisty terrier attacking a perplexed Great Dane.

"Did he have a baseball bat, son?" Pasquin had a slight smile on his face.

"Didn't see none." The joke was lost on Zull who latched the screen behind us. "I'm going back up on the roof to look out for him until the cops get here."

Pasquin and I sat quietly in the kitchen, preparing iced tea and fanning ourselves in the heat. I had given my one electric fan to the workers in the upstairs rooms; we waited for a breeze to come in the windows. It wasn't a breeze, but the sound of sirens—on the road and on the river. Then a helicopter soared overhead, searching the woods for the elusive Bandy. I walked to the porch, where two marked cars had pulled up sharp, their occupants leaping out with guns drawn and moving into the swamp. A sheriff's department patrol boat tied up at the landing, three more cops piling off and filtering through the bushes. It sounded like Miami preparing for a gang war.

"Old Joe gon' think he's pretty important with all this goin' on," Pasquin said as he joined me on the porch. We sat in rockers and waited, listening to the shouting coming from the depths of the swamp. "Cops gon' catch more skeeter bites and nettle burns than criminals out in that swamp. Man like Joe, he knows this swamp too good, is part of it. Nobody gonna catch him out there." He took a slow sip of tea.

"Where do you think he's hiding?" I asked the authority on this swamp.

"Lots of places. Probably staying here, then there, always near water. Dogs can't smell him. Man like that ain't gonna stay put in this swamp. Why, it's possible he's slept in your backyard and mine, and we didn't even know it."

"I don't have a backyard."

"You got a cleared space out back with lumber stacked up and covered with a tarpaulin. How do you know he wasn't there?"

189

Before I could answer, he went on. "And you got an old canoe. He could sleep in there and be out of here before you knew he was even around."

"Pasquin, stop trying to scare me."

"Not doing a thing. Just trying to tell you that you're really in the swamp. Creatures here use each other, bite, scratch, eat, whatever they have to do to survive. The only safe ones are the ones who know the swamp and can prey on others. You and me—we're just intruding guests here. Bandy—he's joined the creatures. My guess is they won't find him until he's rejoined humans and makes a big mistake. He'll do it, too. If that big guy is right and he's on dope, he won't last long."

"The law of the jungle, huh, Pasquin?"

"Yeah. And there ain't no such thing as a human jungle."

The search went on for three hours. Finally, the officers came wearily to their cars and their boat, no Bandy in hand.

Zull stood on the porch, watching in horror as they left. Under his breath, he said, "Damn! If that little shit comes round me again, I'll twist his balls off."

Pasquin and I nodded at each other. We both knew Zull was afraid Bandy was going to do just that to him. The big man wouldn't sleep well tonight.

CHAPTER TWENTY-ONE

Harry MacAllister's grant money came through. He set up a temporary structure at the edge of Palmetto Springs, but close enough for the tour guides to point out the researchers who were mapping the underground caves in the springs. Their hype went on to tell how the scientists would go all the way down the river, exploring and noting facts about the hundreds of underwater caves. "They've found some bodies in these caves recently. Who knows what they may find during this latest research?" The tour boat guide droned out his teasing speculation as he turned the boat where passengers could look into the sinister shadow that formed the opening to the deep main cave.

I rode across the spring in a lifeguard's boat to visit Harry's center of operations.

"I've got two graduate students who dive pretty good, Luanne. Sure you won't join us? I could use you, and it would take you away from the classroom for quite a while."

"Stop teasing me, Harry. I said no before. I'm out of the classroom anyhow, and I want to finish my house."

"Well, keep checking back with me. You may change your mind." He turned to supervise the storage of tanks and scientific instruments in his crude structure.

Seeing the flippers hanging on the walls, along with sophisticated new masks, sent a wave of nostalgia over me. Harry and I had spent a summer in a hut like this, and in ships that permanently housed such equipment. I shook the feeling and turned to go, stopping when I remembered what I came for. "Listen, Amado wants you to be on the lookout for this guy. They suspect he's in the area, armed and scary dangerous." I handed him a copy of an old mug shot of Bandy, taken when he was arrested on one of his drunks.

"Scary dangerous?" Harry winked at me.

"Drugged up to the hilt. Amado says he's likely to hit or shoot at anyone; don't try to catch him yourself."

I turned to leave and ran face first into Vernon. He knew Harry, I was sure, for they both had dived for the sheriff's department, and divers form a sort of bond, like cops. I may have been part of the bonding but only when I was suited up. As a female, I'd probably never be one of their crowd. The two men nodded their greetings, then ignored each other.

Vernon said, "Amado wants you around the office this afternoon. Frank Ellison has agreed to talk. You can sit in the outer room and watch through the two-way."

one

I didn't ask why Tony wanted to let me in on this confession. It had to be more than owing me a favor, but I wanted to hear it bad enough to let him use me for something else. We arrived at the sheriff's office about an hour before they brought Ellison into the holding cell. They planned to take him into a conference room equipped with tapes, microphones, and a video camera.

"Will he have an attorney with him?" I asked Tony.

"Of course. It's his attorney who has convinced him to talk.

He's scared, but I think he'll tell us what we want to know."

"About drugs?"

"About murder. The drug case belongs to the DEA because of the national and international connection. We've got homicides to solve." Tony held the small anteroom door open for us. "Just sit here. Don't turn on any lights. You can talk, but don't shout."

He closed the door and left us in the shadowy room. We were momentarily unable to see anything through the mirror except our own reflections. Then a light clicked on in the other room to reveal a long table with metal chairs. A court reporter set up her machine at one end. Vernon pointed to a corner where a camera looked down on the area, its red light not yet indicating that the proceedings were being filmed.

Tony came in with a tape recorder under his arm and set it up. Then he placed some papers on the table and sat in front of them. Loman followed him with a handcuffed Ellison. A stocky man in his sixties followed them. I assumed that was the lawyer.

"They're not leaving out anything, covering their asses with anything the courts will allow," I whispered to Vernon.

"Okay, Mr. Ellison," Loman spoke unemotionally to Frank, "we'll take off the handcuffs now. Do we have your assurance you won't bolt?"

Ellison nodded, and Loman unlocked the cuffs, placing them in his back pocket. All five people sat down, the reporter pushing away at her keys while looking directly at the person speaking. The red light blinked silently on the ceiling camera.

Tony made the introductions of the people present, calling each name distinctly for the benefit of all the recording devices in the room. Then he faced Ellison whose legs stretched out under the table. He eyed Tony from a slightly lowered head, his face pale. The tan he got from being on the ocean had given way to jail house pallor. The blue prison garb made him look older and shabbier.

"Mr. Ellison, tell us about the day you took Angelina Stephoulous to Pensacola."

Frank stared at him, then shrugged and sat up so he could lean over the table. "She was one horny Greek. Her old man wouldn't let her date even though she had to be pushing thirty. Well, she got even by using a storage room at the seafood company."

"That's the Angel's Bay Seafood Company?"

"Yeah, you know that." He looked for a moment at the recorder, then sneered. "We had a few quickies in that storage room, and just for the record and her old man, I wasn't the first. That broad knew exactly what she was doing."

He looked at his lawyer who nodded, then proceeded. "I had to go to Pensacola to take some tanks to the ship. She wanted to go along, to have what she called a 'tryst' in a motel there. Don't ask me why, but I finally said okay. I told her she'd have to put up with Joe Bandy who was going to ride along with us. He brought along his tool box, said the boss wanted him to help with some heavy work there. Things didn't quite work out like they should've."

"She traveled in your car?" asked Tony.

"Truck. She left her car at a garage for servicing. I picked her up there and took her to work that day." He chuckled lightly. "Her car is still there. I told the guys to hold it until I got back to them. Bet they're scared shitless about now, knowing I'm in the slammer and all."

"You said things didn't work out on the trip. What happened?"

194

Tony was cool, expressionless.

"Bandy was high on something, kept trying to feel her up. She got mad and slapped him around a few times. I laughed at her. Then he got crazy and let something slip, something about getting coke from the tanks and stopping on the beach where all three of us could get high. I think she knew something was going on at the company but now she was in the middle of it. 'Liable,' she said. She got real pissed and said to let her out. Started cursing at me." Ellison sat up and shrugged. "I stopped at a gas station just outside of Pensacola. She piled out and headed for a coffee shop next to the station. I told Bandy to pump the gas while I tried to reason with her. She wouldn't talk to me and was about to make a scene. I thought I'd teach her a lesson, thought maybe if we drove around a while without her, she'd panic and think we really had left her there. Bandy was one mad dude by that time. He'd bought some beer and drank it on top of a couple of snorts. Said we ought to pop her. Anyhow, we drove around the block a few times then went back to the coffee shop. Before we could even get out of the truck, there she was with this old lady. They got into a car and headed back toward Tallahassee on the interstate. That's when I called Petroulious. He was one mad bastard."

"What did he tell you to do?"

The lawyer leaned over and conversed in a whisper with his client, then nodded.

"He said forget the tanks, follow the women and do what's necessary."

The lawyer leaned over again.

"He said to take them out if we had to." Frank lowered his head. This sounded like the defense—just following orders.

"You tailed the women as he said?"

"Over two hundred miles back to Palmetto Springs, then to

195

a house way out in a swamp."

"Ideal, right?" Loman couldn't resist. Tony shot him a look.

"It helped. Made Bandy downright ecstatic. He said we could do anything to them in those woods, that he knew the swamp like the back of his hand. He was snorting more coke by then."

Frank sat back, sighed and looked at the ceiling.

"When did you enter the house, Frank?"

"Bandy saw the lights go on upstairs around nine. He got out and jimmied the door to the kitchen. I followed him inside." Frank had been rehearsed, it seemed, to make sure everyone knew Joe Bandy was the one who actually broke into Carmina's house. "There was this old lady in a downstairs bedroom. She was half undressed when Joe jumped her and threw a towel over her mouth. Scared her bad; she fell flat on the floor. Didn't take long to see she'd never get up. I knew because I saw a heart attack once when an old man died at the market. I wanted to help her, but Bandy pushed me back."

"Yeah, right," Vernon groaned beside me, his face flushed with anger.

"She managed to crawl into the living room and died right there. We heard the rattle from her throat, you know, that sound people make when the life goes out of them."

His lawyer leaned over and whispered again, probably warning him not to embellish the tale.

"Bandy told me to stay downstairs, then he went up to where the lights were on. I heard a couple of cries; he came down with two women, his gun pointed at them."

"Was one woman Angelina Stephoulous?"

"Yeah. She had undressed and was going to sleep that way, I guess. Anyhow she was naked, trying to cover herself with her arms."

"And the other woman was Delia Twiggins?"

"Yeah, I—" He stopped when his lawyer touched his arm.

"I didn't know her. She looked like the old woman Angie got in the car with, but then so did the dead woman. I guess I heard later what her name was." Ellison's eyes darted to the lawyer.

"Go on, what happened then?"

"Bandy tied them to the dining table chairs." He got quiet.

"And?"

"I don't like this part. It's hard to talk about."

The lawyer patted him on the shoulder.

Vernon made a quick snort of disgust. "They got this act down good." I reached over and took his tightly clenched hand.

"Bandy found a bottle of whiskey in one of the cupboards and started guzzling it. Then he found this clothes line over the bathtub. He took a snort of coke, and before I knew it, he had that rope around Angie's neck. She kicked a little and went slack. Bandy turned to me and said, 'piece of cake,' then went around behind that old lady. She had seen what happened to Angie, so she got activated somehow and started moving her chair. She was dancing all over the floor. I guess she bumped the table because a glass fell off and broke on Bandy's foot, cut his ankle. He leaned over to touch it and came up with a handful of blood. That's when he really got crazy. Found a plastic bag and slammed it over her head. Said he was going to let her suffocate slowly, but I guess he didn't get the bag tight enough or there was a hole in it. Anyhow, she didn't show any signs of checking out, and Bandy got tired of waiting. He wrapped that line around the woman's neck twice and strangled her in seconds. He was still dripping blood all over that house; I got a bandage from the bathroom and stopped the bleeding, but he was wild by that time, still sniffing coke and slugging whiskey. Said I'd have to take it from there. Just ran into the swamp and left me there with two dead bodies."

"Poor man," Vernon's hand was cold.

"Frank, did Bandy or you take anything from the house?"

He looked at his lawyer who gave one nod. "Oh yeah, Bandy found this case full of silver dollars. Said he wanted it, but I'd have to keep it for him. Said if I didn't, he'd do the same to me as he did to the women."

"So you kept it?"

Frank nodded. The lawyer asked for a break and some water. Loman recuffed the prisoner and motioned for a uniformed cop to stay in the room. He and Tony left.

Tony joined Vernon and me in the anteroom, "I want you to listen real careful when I question him about the disposal of the bodies. If there is anything you want me to ask, write it on this note pad and give it to the uniform who'll be outside the door."

"Are you looking for anything special?" I asked.

"I don't know if he had help in the springs or not, but I have this hunch he did. You may be able to find out by asking some technical questions. I'd bring you into the room, but the lawyer would have none of it."

Back inside the room, Tony turned on his recorder and again identified everyone.

"Tell us what you did with the bodies, Frank."

"I was in a jam. There was no way I was going to bury them in the swamp or dump them in a sinkhole that night. I didn't know exactly where I was, but I knew the springs were nearby. I thought I'd stow them there until I could find a better place."

"Where did you put them?"

"I found a couple of caves where they could be hidden from most people. Since the trouble with the aquarium grass, divers have to get a permit to go down. I didn't think anyone would be swimming down there. Guess those kids fooled me."

"Current is pretty strong down there. How did you keep them down?"

"Tied them to the pieces of rock jutting from the cave walls."

"With?"

"Fishing line, rope, whatever. I can't even remember now. I was kind of anxious."

"Frank, to drag two bodies into the spring, hide them in two different caves, that must have taken a lot of strength, not to mention time." Amado's comment went without a response; he changed the direction. "What did you do before that? I mean how did you get the bodies to the springs?"

"Yeah. That was something else all right. I had to drag them to the truck, haul them up, then do the same thing, only in the opposite direction, all over again when I got to the springs."

"You said blood was in the house. What did you do about that?"

"Cleaned it up after I got the bodies in the truck. I wiped that place like no cleaning woman ever done."

Loman said nothing, but his sneer screamed "fool!" at Ellison.

"You said it was around nine when you and Bandy got to the house. What time was it when you finished the whole business and headed home?"

"Don't know, maybe close to dawn. I was a mess. I just went home, washed up, and drank my breakfast."

"When did you hear about the boys who found the body?"

Frank was quiet, too quiet. His lawyer looked puzzled but before he could whisper in his ear, Frank offered his explanation. "You know how word travels in that swamp. I heard it from one of my workers, I think. I don't remember which one."

"Then you went back and moved a body?"

"I went down, but when I got close to the surface and saw some people out there in a boat, I took the old lady back down and secured her again. Later that night I cleared her out."

"In the meantime, we found her?"

"Yeah. That woman diver went down and took some pictures."

"How does he know you took pictures?" Vernon turned to me.

I took the pad and wrote a note: *Ask him how he found the space to put two bodies in his truck when it was full of diving tanks.* I opened the door and slipped it to the officer who quietly went in and placed it in front of Tony.

Tony played it cool and waited to ask my question. "Frank, how did you know she took pictures?"

"I was at the hotel. I saw the whole thing, including the kid who went running down there with the camera."

"What happened to the silver dollars you were supposed to save for Bandy?"

"I tied them to the old lady's wrist. They were safe down there, and Bandy wasn't going to do nothing to me as long as I was the only one who could get to them."

"Where are they now?"

Frank was quiet again. "I guess they got away from her wrist. I didn't see them again when I took the body out."

"You took the body out and then what?"

"Stashed it in our old boat until Bandy came and took it to the construction site. Said he had the perfect place, but I guess it wasn't perfect after all."

"And the other body, Angie Stephoulous?"

Frank looked somewhat pained. I couldn't tell if he was faking or not, but Vernon made a disgusted noise and leaned back in his chair. "Now he's going to say he really loved the girl."

"I left her in the cave. No one had found her, and I couldn't risk going back. Then that woman diver found that one, too."

"And the one in the other cave, the one that had been in there longer than the others?"

He looked genuinely startled. He stared first at Tony, then at his lawyer, then finally at the tape recorder. "There's not another body. You're trying to trick me or pin something else on me!"

"Calm down. Frank, tell me how you put those two dead women in your truck when it was full of diving cylinders."

He began to sweat and look to his lawyer for answers. The lawyer faced the detectives and said, "My client has said enough."

"Not enough, sir. He tells all or there's no deal."

The lawyer nodded at Frank, whose hands trembled.

"I found room somehow. I just placed them under a tarpaulin and carried them to the springs."

"The road must have been bumpy through that swamp. Weren't you afraid they'd fall off the truck—resting on top of tanks and all?"

He wiped his forehead with his hand. "Sure I was. But they didn't fall. What are you trying to get me to say?"

"I'm going to ask one last question, Frank. Did you have any help with those bodies after Bandy left the house?"

Frank paled, but he looked straight at Tony and almost shouted, "No!"

With that, the lawyer stood up and said "enough" again, then ordered all recording to stop. Tony didn't stand. He shut off the tape recorder without taking his eyes off Frank. Loman followed his lead and didn't move, either. The reporter finished her typing, shut her machine, and left the room. When the uniformed officer took him away, Frank glanced at his lawyer.

"He'd better be telling the truth, and all of it," said Tony as the lawyer passed his chair. As soon as the door shut, he added, "But he's not. He didn't say a word about the rip in the plastic bag over the lady's head after he put her in the water. And I don't buy that stuff about no help. We're going to have to speak with Mr. Frank Ellison again sometime."

CHAPTER TWENTY-TWO

"Clever, that question about the truck," said Tony as he stirred cream into his coffee. The four of us had walked across the street to a pseudo-Southern cafe where the food ran fast and greasy. Loman ordered a plate of fried-in-cornmeal oysters for everyone.

"You ought to pay her for all this," grinned Vernon.

"He is, at least for the diving part." I laughed. "That's why I signed on as a certified diver, but I'm thinking of charging for all the advice, tea, lemonade and overnight housing of cops."

"I guess Vernon gets to pay double, then." For the first time I saw Tony blush at his own words. He bowed his head and took a sip from his cup.

"I'm paid very well, for your information, sir." Vernon tried not to grin.

Loman stuffed his mouth with oysters, his sleepy eyes never looking up. "Not to change the subject, but why the question about Ellison having help? You think maybe Bandy came back?"

"It's quite a feat if he did it all himself, and there's his brother." Tony turned serious again.

"Jack?" I suggested.

"You're the one who said he pulled a stunt,. stirring up silt and dashing off to a cave." Tony mock-toasted me with his coffee cup.

Zull and his men worked late into the evening to finish the inside wall on the upstairs rooms. He kept finding details to repair, like he didn't want to go home. "I know that guy is out there, ma'am, outside my trailer with a gun." I didn't understand why Joe should want to go after Zull, but the big man harbored deep gut fear. He still wore some bruises from the baseball bat attack.

That night, finally alone, I tried out my brand-new phones, one in the kitchen, one in my new bedroom upstairs. Inhaling the new wood smells, I spoke with Pasquin, then called Vernon. He sounded sleepy, but amused me with long conversation about his past, my past, the springs' past. We didn't speak of the future. Neither of us dared approach the subject of commitment.

My future seemed cast for me when I finally got around to reading my mail and found a letter from the university. I had to come in and fill out papers to return from leave in September. My heart sank. I didn't want to be burdened with student papers and the incessant lecturing on the same topics. I could do it in my sleep, and I was tired of trying to vary the approaches just to hold my own interest. For a mad moment, I thought of accepting Harry's offer to map the spring caves.

In my temporary bedroom, I tried to review some of my linguistics texts, just to see if the old spark could reflame itself. I was deep into the sociolinguistics of a Jewish community in Venice, California, when I realized how quiet it was. As usual my windows were wide open, but no cricket choruses flooded my eardrums, no frogs, no birds. *Someone is outside!*

I moved to another room and peered into the forest from a

window with a better view. Greeted with solid darkness at first, I let my eyes adjust to the fine shadows and intricate designs of a swamp setting. Moss, especially, can play tricks on the eyes; one minute a snake hanging from a vine—which is more than likely a real oak vine hanging from the treetop to the swamp floor; the next a body swinging from a branch, and, if there is enough light, gray lace from a ghost's bridal gown. I caught glimpses of things I could identify—the twisted oak whose branches jutted about like a Siamese dancer, and the tall pine with the rotting top. (Zull said I'd best get rid of that before storm winds blew it onto my brand-new roof.) Thick clumps of sharp-pointed palmetto blocked the passages between the trees. It all blurred into one dark, sound-less barrier.

I retraced my steps to my own room to retrieve my gun and a flashlight. Tiptoeing to a window, I gazed toward the river but saw only darkness in various shades. I waited, then crickets began to sing, and frogs sounded the all-clear. Maybe it was only a fox or an elusive Florida panther, even a black bear that sometimes ap-pears in these parts.

I breathed deeply, then turned on the flashlight and moved it around the walls in this room Zull had been working on all day. Knotty cypress wood paneled the walls from floor to ceiling. Acoustic tiles had been fitted overhead. I lifted the flashlight a second time to the tiles. Zull had placed metal strips evenly to hold the tiles in place, then eased the white rectangles over the strips. Something wasn't right in one corner. The white tile looked stained, maybe broken. I pulled up a work bench and reached for the tile. Unable to reach it, I found a broom in the hall, and with the handle, poked at the tile. It bounced up and over a few times, then hit the floor with a thud, and another thud. I looked down at the bottom of the bench. Two pieces of broken white tile lay on the floor along with a small black case.

Placing the flashlight on the floor, I knelt to pick up the case. I knew what it was before I got off the bench, but I shook it for confirmation. The jingle of heavy coins sounded like a police alarm, and the hair stood on my neck. No wonder Zull was afraid of Joe Bandy. I opened the case, and there they were—the Carmina Twiggins inheritance—twenty-five silver dollars. They were worth a lot today, but enough to murder for? Maybe for a guy like Joe Bandy. What was Zull doing with them? All these questions took a back seat to the realization that they were stored in my house, and just maybe Joe knew that. He had come here to attack—what? Maybe it was Zull he was after all the time.

I tucked the case of silver dollars under my mattress, then returned to the other room and, with the broom handle and a lot of stretching, readjusted the broken tile in the ceiling.

Checking all the downstairs doors and windows, I heard the crickets sing again. In my dreams, I saw a crazed Joe Bandy sitting in the old oak outside my window, watching, waiting, and sniffing.

Zull and his men appeared early the next morning to begin work on the last room upstairs, the one I intended to use as an office. I stood on the landing, sipping coffee, as they carried up more cypress paneling. While the others worked in the small room, I noticed Zull sneak into the room he had completed. I watched from the doorway. He looked up at the tile, then climbed onto the bench and touched his fingertips to the stained end. That's when I realized I had replaced the tile backwards. The stain was at the opposite end, and Zull knew it. He paled as he stared upwards.

"Anything wrong?" I asked innocently enough.

He jumped, then stepped down from the bench. "That tile is stained. I'll have to get you another one."

I pretended to inspect it for the first time. "You're right, and please do get another one."

He rushed from the room to give specific instructions to his crew, then said he wanted to do some additional inspection of the roof. I sat on the porch and watched him haul his long ladder to the carport, then climb across to the house roof. Without being too conspicuous, I left the porch and took a walk to the landing. From there I could see Zull's thick body balancing on top of the house; one foot on each side of the pitched roof, a pair of field glasses in hand, he scoured the forest. Satisfied that Joe Bandy wasn't anywhere around, he crawled down, went to his truck and pulled out a white acoustic tile. I knew he would go back upstairs, and in privacy remove the stained one. I wondered what he would do when the black case didn't fall out.

It was time to call Amado. I went to the kitchen where the workers wouldn't hear me. Upstairs, I heard pounding and the shouting of orders as my office came together. I picked up the phone. No dial tone. I checked the outlet. Everything looked okay, but the phone was dead. Maybe the workers had done something upstairs. I found a dead phone there, too. I ran outside to the new pole erected near the rutted road. Following the wires, I traced them to the side of the house. Cut clean. That's why the crickets went quiet last night!

"Can you make a call to the sheriff on your radio?" I asked a construction worker. He obliged me, and I gave Tony the particulars of the night. The worker stood wide-eyed, then mumbled "You're welcome," when I thanked him for the radio.

The house with its building noises made me nervous. The landing seemed a better spot to wait for the law. I measured time by the laps against the marshy shore, watching tadpoles dart like sperm through their watery world, hoping the stick-like crane wouldn't come along and swallow them whole. It did come. Its pointed beak stabbed the water like a murderer's knife, slicing the life away from the nervous amphibians.

CHAPTER TWENTY-THREE

I leaned against the sturdy old post that held up the few
boards left at the landing. Swamp sounds created a surreal chorus
in my head. Then it all came together like a delayed explosion. A
desperate, evil, unceasing scream sounded from the forest, in-
creasing in volume as its source moved closer. From inside the
house, a male voice hollered, "Joe Bandy!" Zull's big body climbed
out an upstairs window onto the roof. From the rutted road, I
could hear cars and see dust. The cops were on their way.

Bandy exploded out of the forest, his wiry little body a
bouncing ball of irritation, his eyes wide. I ran to the edge of the
road, still within the cover of trees. Bandy turned my way several
times, and like an animal seemed to sense my presence. But the
urge to get Zull pulled at him like a magnet, and he turned toward
the house. He kept screaming, primal threats that were pure sound.
Zull had taken refuge on the roof, an act he regretted the minute
Bandy spotted him and pulled out a pistol. He fired indiscrimi-
nately at the house. Windows cracked and chips flew from the
roof. Zull ducked around the other side, and I hit the ground.
Swamp mud plastered my face, arms, and chest. The sticky palmetto in front of me provided the only barrier. I didn't dare run
back to the landing.

When the cavalry finally arrived, they darted behind open

car doors, guns drawn. Bandy had seen them first. Tossing his empty pistol into the underbrush, he dived under the steps, squirming on his belly like a lizard. He screamed something about killing cops and Zull. Then his scream changed. A tone of surprise and fear, then quiet until he came running from the house, covering his face with one hand, raising the other in the air.

"Get me a doctor! A snake bit me!"

Good old moccasin! I knew I let you live under there for a reason. I imagined Bandy crawling for his life and meeting that deadly black head straight on. Down on the ground like that, hemmed in, the snake would have taken the only action nature provided him—strike! Running isn't an option now.

I looked under the house while a cop called for paramedics on a patrol car radio. In the shadows, I wasn't sure, but I thought I saw a long black movement toward the swamp on the other side.

When Bandy had been carted away, Tony had all the workers sit on the porch and give statements to the deputies. Loman busied himself with Bandy's gun and looking about the yard for bullet casings. Zull, Tony, and I sat at the kitchen table. I placed the black zipper case of silver dollars in the middle. Zull breathed deeply, then his eyes watered.

"Mr. Zullinger, I'm going to read you your rights in case we decide an arrest needs to be made. I want you to realize you don't have to talk to us." Zull nodded, and Tony went through the Miranda reading.

"How did you come by these silver dollars?"

Zull's eyes watered even more, and for a moment I thought the oversize man would break into sobs. He gulped in a long breath and composed himself, then folded his hands on top of the table and talked.

"I knew Bandy was up to something, too jittery on the job. Couldn't get him to do anything right. He'd been on drunks before, but this was different—too nervous, always jumping when somebody got near him, shooting off his mouth in some angry argument for just about nothing. He'd got himself a lot of coke somewhere and had his pinky up his nose most of the time. What we pay him for construction work won't get him a supply like that. I figured he'd been stealing money again. Then we found that woman in the cement at the hunt camp. Nobody but Bandy would stoop that low. Anyhow, I noticed him carrying a sack one day. He often did that, said it was his lunch, his daily supply of cheap whiskey." Zull tried to snicker. It came out like a sob. "But he kept the sack too close to him. I gave him an order to load some cement chunks once, then watched him stash the sack behind some bricks. While he was busy, I looked in the sack and found that." He pointed to the case on the table. "There was a bottle of Jack Daniels and, believe it or not, a sandwich, in that sack. I took the case and replaced the sack behind the bricks. At the end of the day, he grabbed the sack and made a quick look. He went wild, saying I stole his money. He never said silver dollars in a black case, just that he had money in the sack and it was gone. He said, 'I'll rip your throat out for this, Zull. Your lard will be all over the county!' The other workers ran him off, but I knew he'd make good on those threats. I had that body in the cement to remind me he was capable of anything."

"Why not return the case to him?" Tony asked.

"Are you kidding! He'd have chopped off my hand when I handed it to him. I hid it in several places before we got this job. He came after me that first time, but mostly he busted up your house, Ms. Fogarty. Sorry."

"Do you know how much danger you put Ms. Fogarty in

when you hid those coins in this house?" Tony looked directly at the man.

"Didn't think much about that at the time. I figured anybody was in danger when Bandy was on a high. I saw him tear up a dog once. He was harassing some people down on the river, wanted to use their boat and they wouldn't let him. He starts screaming and making threats. They had a little dog that barked, then nipped him on the ankle. He grabbed that mutt and twisted his head back until it broke, then stomped on the animal. Me and the husband ran him off with a couple of boards. Little kids screamed for hours over that dog. Cops arrested Bandy. Sent him up a few days for drunk and disorderly. Man's a fucking wildcat murderer—sorry, ma'am."

"Wasn't too smart to steal from a murderer, right?" Tony said.

"Dumbest thing I ever done, sir."

Tony warned Zull to stay around, to see a lawyer as there was a possibility he could still be arrested. In the meantime, the deputies would check out all his alibis for the week of the murders.

"One last question. Did you have any connection with Frank Ellison? Ever do any construction work for him?" Tony said.

"Lots. His boss owned the company I worked for. Never did any independent of that company."

"Ever help him with other things, like diving or carrying heavy equipment?"

Zull shook his head, looking surprised. "I can't even swim."

"Okay, stay put."

Joe Bandy gave the hospital hell. His face swollen to the size of a basketball, he cried for drugs, sweating in pain for cocaine, getting antivenom instead. He had loud nightmares that woke the other patients, shouting how thousands of black snakes swam out of the water to grab him. Sedation rarely calmed him for more than an hour. Three detectives sat in his room in shifts and listened to all this. Officially, Bandy was under arrest, although it was doubtful he understood that. His court-appointed lawyer came in frequently, shaking his head from the futility of trying to communicate. As soon as the doctors could get his mind back together, the detective on watch would charge him with attempted murder on Zull, property destruction on my house, and the murders of Angelina Stephoulous and Delia Twiggins.

In the meantime, I trusted Zull enough to continue work on my house, and to repair the damage Joe had done with his gun. When the pounding and paint fumes got too much, I pulled out the old canoe stowed behind the house and rowed down the river. *paddled*

In early August, the river gets lazy, like an over-full diner. The summer rains swell it until its banks lose stretches of shoreline. With water pouring in from underground springs, its currents seem to slow up, to say "I'm satiated." September will bring the storms, hurricane season. Now is the time to enjoy the river's calm, its lush vegetation overhanging in a canopy. In some spots, willows dip their tips into the sluggish current, conjuring up visions of Scarlett O'Hara in one of her wide, lacy gowns. I lazed in the canoe, letting it drift. It drifted right to the cabin owned by people from Alabama.

paddle Using one oar, I held it against the decking post and let the canoe ease up until I could see the watery darkness beneath the wooden structure. The boat I had seen before was still there, wedged against the back posts, but not tied. Bending as low as possible, I pushed under partway, but I didn't want to get stuck and have to climb out and stand in mud up to my butt. Instead, I lifted an oar to the underside of the deck to push back when I caught a glimpse of something shiny tucked into the boards above me.

"A tank!" It had been wedged tightly between the floor of the deck and two cross-wise support beams. Moving closer, I could see the rust, and then the circular cut near the top. It had to be one of Ellison's, and maybe it was full.

I rowed hard against the current. If anyone had seen me come here, they might remove the tank before I called Amado. My arms ached when I crawled onto my own landing, then took off running through the puddles and damp grass, splattering my ankles with muddy freckles.

"I wonder what you'll find next in these swamps," said Tony as he watched Vernon and another detective edge beneath the deck in my canoe and remove the tank. Vernon slipped from the canoe into the stowed boat and rowed out behind the other man. Coming close to the bank, two uniformed men grabbed both boats and dragged them across the muddy foliage to solid ground. All four men wore gloves to preserve any prints, and the two crime scene men wasted no time in dusting for them.

"Loman's getting a search warrant for this place. The people in Alabama don't want it torn apart, but if we find drugs in that tank, they aren't going to have a choice."

After a deputy lifted all possible prints from the tank, Vernon held the top part in his hands while his fellow officer held the bottom and twisted. The rust gave way, and the top pulled loose.

"Full!" said Vernon. The other detective slanted the tank so

Tony could reach inside. He pulled out a small square packet filled with white powder. Slicing through the oilskin and plastic, he removed a tiny bit of powder which he tapped into a small clear bag with three ampoules. Sealing the bag, he leaned over the side of the tank and crushed the first ampoule. The liquid inside blued with a slight stir. He crushed the second ampoule, then the third. Both turned pink when their chemical mixed with the cocaine.

"That's the stuff, all right," he said. "Bag it. Now we wait." He gave an order for the deputy to find Loman and tell him, "The stuff is here, lots of it."

I sat in my canoe downriver and watched the search. Plastic-gloved men kept coming out of the shabby cabin with filled bags. Vernon and two other men searched the deck, on top and underneath. Finally, Tony walked through the bushes to my spot in the murky shallows.

"We found an open packet inside the house. My guess is this is the tank Bandy stole when Ellison made the complaint against him. He didn't want the complaint followed up when he realized what was in the tank. Bandy had found himself a glory hole of coke. Seven bottles of high-priced liquor lined the counter in the kitchen—one for each day of the week. I'm guessing again that Bandy cashed in a silver dollar or sold some coke and bought the good stuff. We got a lot of prints, and I'd near 'bout bet my grannie's life they're Bandy's." Tony glanced at me through river reeds, then smiled, "You done good, girl." For him, that was an emotional academy award.

I sat in my house, its broken windows and roof nicks repaired, the phones back in service. Vernon had a meeting to attend. When I started to complain about his working overtime for Tony, he stopped me. "It's a special kind of meeting, Luanne. Tony has nothing to do with it." AA flashed through my mind.

I was blue as they say in New Orleans. Not because of the highs and lows surrounding this case, but bluer than blue about going back to work. I wanted to do something else, but I had put in too much time, had too much at stake, to leave it now. I had a solid retirement fund, but was nowhere near retirement age. I could see in front of me almost as many years as I left behind, with none of the attendant sparks of discovery, the stimulation I had felt as a graduate teaching assistant. Stayed too long at the fair, Luanne—so they say. Pasquin interrupted my misery.

"More nastier business in this swamp I've never seen, Miss Fogarty," he said as he grunted into a rocking chair. "Never had this problem before, even when that Jones clan tried to rob the ships going down the river."

"When was that?"

"Nineteen, oh, thirty, maybe. Been pretty peaceful ever since."

We rocked, sipped tea, then I let a tear drop in Pasquin's view.

"Just like your mama, cry for just about nothing. You happy or sad? She cried for both, too."

I wiped the tear away. "You knew her well."

"Um."

"I've got a great job in the scheme of things, Pasquin. Why do I not want to go back to it?"

"No challenge to you anymore. Let me tell you, I never had that problem with this river. Always something different staring you in the face—weather, insects, currents. Lordy! I'm glad I stuck with it." He slapped his hat on his knee. "Let's drive over to Mama's Table and eat all she's got!"

He was right. A big platter of grouper fingers fried in cornmeal, a steaming bowl of cheese grits, and nine hushpuppies piled on top, with a side of sugary cole slaw, brought me out of the dumps and into cholesterol camp. We bought a whole bottle of white wine and slowly washed down the river comfort. Full as ticks, we didn't even try to resist the coconut custard pie foisted on us when Mama sang its praises. "Best in the South," she cooed as she held it next to the table. "Been in the refrigerator only two hours, nice and cool, but fresh." We nodded, unable to speak.

We drank three cups of coffee. Pasquin insisted on adding some sweet liqueur that Mama brought in from the New Orleans French Quarter, pronounced *N'Or-lay-awns* in Cajun. I grew mellow, my blues swallowed with the cuisine.

"I loved your mama. One of the best friends I ever did have."

I nodded. How much love had he shown her? My father must have read those papers. If he didn't ask, then what did it matter that my mother might have taken some pleasure where she could find it when her real love was not around?

Loman interrupted us. His sleepy eyes danced along with a low chuckle. Sitting beside me in the booth, he said, "Know that boarder your cousin had, Mr. Pasquin?" He stopped to chuckle again. "We escorted him to her house. Said he needed to get some shirts and stuff. Guess he didn't think we'd look inside the suitcase he brought. Took his shirts all right. Got some ladies' silk drawers, too. Confessed to wearing the things. We compared the sizes, and they didn't belong to your cousin." Loman couldn't contain himself and squeezed the lids shut. His belly heaved with laughter. "Buys the things himself. Still had the price tags attached."

217

CHAPTER TWENTY-FOUR

Dressed in tailored cotton slacks and a silk blouse, I felt like those women in the fifties who wore gloves, hats, and hose to work. I opened the car door, lumbered up the steps of the modern brick building, then took a deep breath. The linguistics department air-conditioning was frigid, like me at the moment. I waited for the Chair to sign the papers that would assign me at least three classes of undergraduates in the Fall.

"If you plan to publish we can limit your load this year. Anything going?" The Chair wore rimless glasses. A leftover from the sixties, his stringy hair grazed his neck. Something in Celtic blazed across his dirty sweatshirt. A bald spot topped off the whole image. Once a boy genius, he had published volumes of South American Indian dialects, using transformational grammar. In those days, angry with his country, he had spent most of his time wandering the jungles and mountains of Brazil and Peru, living off graduate grants. At fifty-plus, he found himself a university bureaucrat, doling out class schedules, granting leaves, and goading professors to publish. The job suited him now, his noble nights in the insect-infested Indian villages just as much a part of history as the bullet-infested villages of Southeast Asia he had avoided.

"MacAllister asked me to help him map the caves on the

Palmetto River, but I doubt this department would see that as publishing." I watched his eyes dart behind the glasses. He never looked at me straight on.

"You could write a book about it, but where would language fit in?"

That was a no from him. He guarded the gates of educational propriety, knowing where he was safe from having to head back into those jungles of publishing.

"There is something that might work," I said suddenly, kicking myself for even thinking of it. "There was at one time a Cajun—Acadian—community in this city. Not many people left, but I'd like to trace their origins, with their language patterns being the center, of course."

"Marvelous! Get me a proposal, will you? We need to beef up publishing in this department."

I wanted to say, "Then why not write something yourself?" He'd never own up that he was as burned out as I was on the stuff.

"In the meantime, here's your Fall schedule. Get your book list in right away."

I left the campus. Once a thrill to me, I had mourned for it when I graduated with a bachelor's degree. One semester of high school English teaching, and I returned. Scholarships and Daddy, thank you! The idea of Cajuns in this part of the south intrigued me, but writing a proposal? My stomach churned at the thought of convincing my "superiors" in accepted proposal language that I should be freed from students to pursue "research." I looked at my schedule; two classes in basic phonetics, one in the historical origins of the romance languages. Dear God!

I stopped by the sheriff's office on the way home. Maybe to find an outlet in murder and mayhem. Instead, I found Loman and Tony sharing a pizza.

"Vernon's at the crime lab, if that's who you're looking for," Tony said. He held out the box. "Had lunch?"

"Tony, is there a place on this force for a diver?"

"If Jack's position doesn't hold up, there will be, why?"

"Just wondered." I leaned over and helped myself to a wedge of dripping tomato, cheese, and pepperoni.

"Are you looking for a position on the diving team?" Loman stopped mid-chew.

I shrugged. Tony put down his lunch and wiped his hands. "Sorry. To be a diver you also have to be an officer. Like Vernon. He's out on a handwriting thing right now. Nothing to do with diving. You want to join the force, go through the training to become a deputy."

"At my age?" I sounded whiny inside my head.

The men looked at each other, then grabbed more pizza.

"Look, I don't really want to be on the force," I said. "I just don't want to go back to teaching. I'm looking for sympathy."

"Tell you what," Tony wiped his mouth, "when we question Jack, I want you in the anteroom again. We're going to ask him to retrace that dive with you, and if he's lying, I want to know. Does that help any?"

But they held off questioning Jack, hoping his brother would slip up or implicate him somehow. Thus far, neither he nor Joe Bandy was talking; it became a waiting game.

For two days, I lived the life I had planned when I moved back into the old house. Scrubbing walls in preparation for painting, washing the salvageable screens, cutting back the vegetation that threatened to move in with me. I forgot about the change in the p/f sounds from Latin to Spanish, French, Portuguese, Rumanian, and Italian, refusing to be drawn into planning lectures I had repeated for years.

The same day my upstairs rooms were being painted antique white, I got the call to go in and listen to Jack. Tony had grilled his brother with no results until he told him about Jack's fingerprint on one of the tanks and on a trash can out back of Carmina's house. Frank cracked, broke down and cried about betraying his brother who, he said, had only come when he called for help. Tony really hadn't found Jack's fingerprints anywhere.

I sat, again, with Vernon in the anteroom where we watched Jack and Tony exchange glares. The court reporter's back faced the mirror. Jack's lawyer sat at his side, and Loman stood in the corner. Tony pushed the play button and read Jack his rights.

"Your brother has implicated you in the disposal of the bodies of Angelina Stephoulous and Delia Twiggins. Do you have anything you want to say about that?"

Jack looked at his lawyer who nodded.

"He called me late that night. Said he got into a mess with Joe Bandy, that Joe had killed two people in a drug craze. My first instinct was to send deputies out there, but Frank convinced me that other people would kill him if he got caught. Drug people. Anyhow, I went out there, found three dead women inside this swamp house, and helped him with the bodies. We put two of them in my station wagon. Since the third one died of a heart attack, we left her there. I guess in some insane moment of deranged reasoning we decided the spring caves would hide the bodies until we could put them where they'd never be found, possibly in the Gulf. We hauled them to the edge of the spring on the swamp side, then Frank drove to Fogarty Spring and got the old motorboat. We suited up in the dark, dragged the bodies, one by one, into the water and tied them in the caves. The old lady wouldn't stay put with the fishing line. I had to wrap an old fan belt around her neck. They could have stayed there for months if it hadn't been for those kids. When we went back, Frank freaked at something just as he got the fan belt off. Then Luanne Fogarty went down and found the woman. Later that night, we slipped in from the other side and took the old lady's body to the other side of the tour boats. Frank had tied up the motor boat there. We had to row it for miles with that dead woman between our feet before we dared use the engine. I got out at the Fogarty Spring dock. Frank said he was meeting Bandy somewhere near the hunt camp and they'd handle things from there. Said I ought to forget what happened. I tried." Jack shrugged.

"When you went down with Luanne, you tried to distract her. Why?" Tony glanced toward the two-way mirror.

"Those damn silver dollars. Frank had cut them loose when he tried to get the old lady out of the cave the first time. He said Bandy insisted on keeping them, but Frank was scared to death they'd be found in his possession. I hid them in the other cave, in a little niche I'd found on an earlier dive. I didn't want Luanne to find it and distracted her long enough to place it in my diving bag. By then, Bandy went crazy, even threatened to tell the law that Frank had killed the women to steal their silver dollars. To shut him up, Frank arranged to meet him at the hunt camp with the coins." Jack stopped abruptly, his eyes down, but his head held high.

"Do you plan to charge my client?" asked the lawyer, breaking the silence. All the deputies in the room knew the tragedy—a law man gone bad.

"Yes," said Tony and began to read off the list of felony charges. With an expression of profound hurt, Loman cuffed his former colleague and led him to a holding cell.

"That's it, then," I said as I turned to Vernon.

"That's it for the Ellison brothers, Joe Bandy, and the drug smugglers—at least the ones they caught. This'll be some trial for this town." He squeezed my shoulder.

On the way out, we met a deputy escorting a sheepish Rentell, his bony wrists clasped in plastic handcuffs. As he opened the door, the deputy turned and grinned at us, flashing an evidence bag full of pink and black panties. "Shoplifting," he mouthed.

Pasquin sat with me on the porch, watching the twilight over the river and fanning away the muggy afternoon. I told him the story of Rentell and his stash of panties. He stopped fanning when I finished.

"Guess it was just in the cards for my cousins to die at the hands of violence. Joe Bandy, now that's a bad sort." He fanned again, rocked, and leaned his head back on the woven reeds of the chair. "Knew a fellow once, in the thirties, who liked to put on those loose silky underpanties women wore back then. Kept stealing them out of his sister's dresser drawer. Said it gave him the best feeling around his loins, tickled them he said." He stopped suddenly, his cheeks puffed out with air. A chuckle rose from deep in his throat. He finally let go with an old man's cackle. The crickets stopped their preparation for the night's concert. The moment caught, and we howled until tears ran down our cheeks. I hadn't laughed this hard since before Daddy died.

Late at night, my house smelled of new paint and lumber, keeping me awake along with the insect and amphibian sounds from outside my open windows. The creaks and groans of its oldness made me jump at every sound, but I told myself the bad guys were in jail; I was safe. It didn't work. Restless, I roamed around the upstairs rooms then headed for the lower floor. It needed repair, and if Zull could stay out of jail, maybe he would be around here a little longer. Standing at the screen, I relished the slight breeze that brought in the fecund smell of the swamp floor. A bull frog again stood center stage on the front steps and croaked as though he had a microphone. "Watch your language, old frog. My snake may get hungry."

I headed for the kitchen. I wanted it completely redone, country style, of course, but with modern sinks and appliances. No more hand washing the dishes. Turning on the light, I filled the kettle. I waited for it to boil, thinking of how my kitchen would look, when I spied a three-inch cockroach—palmetto bug—scooting across the old linoleum, its shiny brown back carried above skinny, hair-lined legs. Front feelers guided its path. I waited until it came close to the counter, then reached across and opened the back door. Shoving it gently with my foot, I turned it outdoors where it disappeared into decaying leaves. Looking at the dark forest through the screen, I wondered about my snake. I hoped he was safe, that some radar-eyed owl hadn't eaten him for supper. The tea kettle whistled, jarring me back into the human world.

CHAPTER TWENTY-FIVE

Things had to be worked out with the trial. The feds and the locals were "discussing" what to do and where to do it. The DEA had busted a huge smuggling outfit that involved several fishing companies besides Arno Petroulious'. Frank languished in prison, depressed over implicating his brother. The guards had him on suicide watch. Joe Bandy displayed his defiance and had to be hauled everywhere in tight chains. He couldn't keep his mouth shut in public, screaming frame-ups and vowing to get the bastards—whoever they might be. Vernon said his lawyer feigned upset but was actually encouraging this behavior. They were looking to an insanity plea based on the effects of drugs and alcohol.

I was on trial, too. Two weeks to go before my first lecture of the school term. Pasquin sat on my porch and said, "It's gon' be real hard getting to that university when it rains on the rutty road. You gon' be late lots of times. 'Course I could take you to Fogarty Spring in the boat and you could catch a ride with somebody there."

Then Tony would add, "You better go back to your day job, Luanne. Little payment for diving every now and then; won't keep you in construction workers."

Zull, who had not yet been arrested, hinted, "This kitchen

will be a show piece! Just you wait and see. I owe you one, Ms. Fogarty, and this will prove just what I can do."

Vernon didn't help when he squeezed my hand and said, "I'll see you in the evenings, keep your mind off things."

But Harry was the worst. He came by twice to tell me his graduate divers needed more training in this kind of watery terrain. His offer had a nice carrot on the end. "You'll keep your regular salary, you know."

I sat on the floor, searching through the box where I had placed my lecture tablets. If I was going back to work, I'd better get to it or I'd look like a fool. A brisk coolness blew through the front screen, less muggy. When I walked around outside, the leaves crunched rather than sank under my feet. Fall showed itself all around me. My skin felt comfortable, but I missed the prickliness of heat and sweat on oily skin, of watery beads forming at the nape of my neck and dripping down my back. That uncomfortable southern humidity brought this part of the world alive, forced all the living things—safe or not—into the open. I thought of my snake. He would head back into a hole somewhere when he wasn't swimming in the river. I owed that snake. Hell! The entire sheriff's department owed that snake.

Someone knocked at the screen door, jarring me from my nostalgia. I opened the screen for Tony. "I haven't seen you in several days now," I said.

"It's Jack Ellison," Tony looked weary, "he's jumped bail."

"And you just happen to come by here to tell me this?"

"We've been searching the area, asking people if they've seen him. His diving equipment disappeared from his house along with him. When his brother gave him away, he went into severe depression. For a few nights, we had both brothers on suicide watch, but Jack seemed to come out of it. Looked downright happy when the judge set bail."

I sat in the approaching twilight after Tony left. Darkness appeared earlier, blocking the river view first, then blacking out all vegetation. The swamp emitted a deadness not present during the long summer season. Pasquin still dropped by but left earlier now. Soon he wouldn't stay after three when the air would get too chilly. On cold days he wouldn't come at all. Of course, I'd be at work most days. The grand funk had me by the neck.

I busied myself in the old kitchen, cooking up a meat stew, *N'Or-lay-awns* style. As I washed onion fumes from my burning eyes, I heard a voice at the screen door. "Smell's great! Can I have some?"

Vernon's muscular form filled up the screen area. We had not been able to see much of each other, the complaint of most cop wives and sweethearts. I had convinced myself I knew their plight, their dedication, and I wouldn't be a complainer.

We ate stew, sitting on pillows in the living room, a candle burning on a sofa table. The old fireplace was still boarded over, waiting for Zull to do his brick art. In the meantime, the place resembled a hippie pad from the sixties—Asian rug, lots of pillows in the middle of the floor, furniture pushed against the walls. But, it wasn't the sixties. My wisps of gray and Vernon's missing strands testified to that. And the floor got hard too quickly, the candles gave insufficient light to see what we were eating. And no wine, for Vernon's sake.

"You could at least put on some sitar music," he laughed.

"Can't. My sitar is on records; I have a CD player now."

"So our karma has come to this—hairless, recordless, half-blind wonders!"

"Yeah, aging hippies who prefer a nice soft mattress to this hard floor," I whispered as we both fell backwards in laughter, upending empty stew bowls and throwing soup spoons across the room.

He stayed the night and we forgot our tell-tale gray hairs and bones that didn't like hard floors. We didn't need sitar music or any of the accompanying drugs. We had lived through the era, our senses intact, our priorities of bodily pleasures played out on a Beautyrest with crisp white sheets, and a rocking good chorus of crickets and frogs to keep us in the mood.

Vernon said good-bye before dawn. He pecked me on the ear. When I heard him shut the front door, I rolled into his spot and savored his warmth and the remnant smell of his body. Lulled back to sleep, it was ten before I opened my eyes again. A gentle autumn rain tapped on the palmetto bushes. I was tempted to stay there all day, to grab some coffee and a good book and not even get dressed. Facing the windows, I noticed rain beginning to blow inside and dampen the table there. I gave up the womb-like covers for slippers and a flannel shirt.

I stood in front of the closed window, staring outside. Two bright red cardinals flitted about, oblivious of the wet. Three frogs hopped into view, then sat on a piece of lumber in the back yard. The rain pounded harder on their backs. It must be glorious to feel that water all around you, little froggies, like going back to the tadpole state... A feeling shook me. Water—going back to origins.

I slipped into my bathing suit, then struggled with the wetsuit. Downing a full glass of water, I ran into the rain and loaded my diving gear into the Honda. I had little patience with the road's mud-filled ruts. I bumped along, nearly blowing a tire on a piece of rotted log. The rain fell harder. *At least it's not lightning!* I pulled into the Palmetto Springs lot, empty this early in the morning and this late in the season. Grounds workers stared at me as I yanked out tank, flippers, and mask, then one offered to help carry everything to the dock.

My agitation frightened the man who finally asked, "Is there more trouble in the springs, ma'am?"

"Look, call Detective Amado. You remember him from the murder cases, right? Tell him to get here, that I've gone diving in the spring."

He nodded, his eyes wide with excitement. His face was the last thing I saw before jumping feet first into deep water off the floating dock.

Ice water engulfed me as I let my buoyancy drop slowly to the depths. Then I went horizontal and propelled toward the far cave, my flippers doing most of the work. I was in a wide section of the spring, white limestone all around me. To my left I could see the small cave where we had found the skeleton of the unidentified girl. I wasn't headed there. Moving at an angle, face first, I swam deeper until I reached the small opening and the ledge where Angie Stephoulous had rested in her underwater hideout. I had to slow down to maneuver myself through the opening, then sped up as I entered the wide cavern. Halfway across, I arranged my buoyancies. I needed to remain stationary with as much space between my head and the top of the cave as between my feet and the bottom, kind of like a satellite in space. I remained very still to look all around me. My light was good for maybe ten feet. It revealed only more limestone walls in the distance. Then I spotted something dark directly below and in front of me. Attempting to keep the light shining on it, I swam to where the opposite wall curved into the floor of the cave. A diving tank! A newer model and no cut around the top. The gauge showed over three-quarters full of air left. I shone the light up the wall until I spied the the tunnel that led to Hollowell Sink. Dreading, yet knowing, what I would see, I edged through the opening. I swam almost to the end when my light picked up what I knew was there all along. Jack Ellison in a fetal position. He grasped his mask in one hand and his flippers were still on his feet. He floated lifeless, bumping against the rocky wall with each small wake. His eyes were open, but he saw nothing. The two strands of green eel grass that waved back and forth across his face, mocking this human intruder, had more life than he did.

We decided it would be easier to remove Jack's body from the sink. Vernon and I entered from the spring side and pushed him out the tunnel where two other divers caught him in their body basket.

"We found a note on his slate, in his diving bag still around his waist. He had ruined his life by helping his brother, he said, and he couldn't stand the thought of spending years in prison. Said he couldn't see much future even if he did get out." Tony spoke to all the divers at a picnic table in Hollowell Sink Park. "Luanne, meet me back at the office."

Vernon deposited me in Tony's cluttered office, then went off to file his report. I waited nearly an hour, trying to drink the dark brew Amado had cooking in his coffee pot. All that diving made me hungry and thirsty. I was about to leave for the cafe across the street when he came in, dragging two deputies behind him.

"What's the state lab say about her?" Tony asked one of the men.

"Her teeth don't match any records of any missing girls. She has no sign of trauma on any of the bones, and your divers didn't find a knife or any other kind of weapon in the area. They don't know who the hell she is." The exhausted deputy spoke with the frustration of years of dead ends.

"What do they plan to do now?" Tony tossed some folders on the floor and claimed his seat.

"Reconstruct. The artist starts next week. They're pretty sure she's white and young. Lab says they got DNA from a tooth. In the meantime, me and Bozo here are going to keep on checking out missing persons."

"Yeah, well you and Bozo and the other clowns do a mighty fine job." Tony turned to me, dismissing the two men.

"It's that other body—bones—you found. No connection with the Ellison thing. We may never identify her. She'll join the hundreds of others in these files—dead bodies, no names." He waved to a table behind his desk and flipped through the curling edges of some folders.

"Identified two, arrested God knows how many," I said. "What's one you can't solve?"

"I get paid to solve them all! It's this unfinished stuff that gets to me. And then some killer gets off because of a courtroom technicality. I get so damn tired of this shit!" He pounded his fist on top of more files on his desk. The face flamed red, and his hair actually fell onto his forehead.

I smiled in triumph. "Now you sound like me. I tell you what, you go lecture on the fine points of Middle English grammar, and I'll find the crooks."

"Okay, okay." Tony clasped his hands in front of his chest. Looking directly at me, he said, "You really did this, girl. Your poppa would be proud." He leaned forward, still looking at me. "You know you're going to get all kinds of commendations, from this department, from the community, hell! probably even from the federal government! And you know what, you deserve every one of them!"

231

"Do you think you could give me yours right now in the form of a fried fish plate?"

He smiled, stood, and offered me his arm. We headed across the street. "You're easy, girl."

"Don't call me girl."

We found the cafe nearly empty and did it justice with the full platter—fried flounder, hush puppies, cheese grits, spiced apples, and bourbon whiskies.

"This place has probably killed more people than a hundred Joe Bandy's," said Tony.

CHAPTER TWENTY-SIX

I pulled my heavy sweater-coat around my shoulders as I finished the hot, lemony tea Mama served us. Pasquin had filled his with sugar and cream; tea-au-lait he called it. January at Mama's Table was dismal. The vacation crowds waited inside their homes for the hot summer to pull them to the cool springs again. Not even men from the hunt camp came by this season, because no hunt camp existed on this river anymore. The courts closed the property and held it in limbo as evidence in the drug trial. The venue was moved to Jacksonville. But no one else connected with the crime had been moved there yet. It would take months to get everything just right. Not a single one of the arrested got bail. "Too likely to flee the country, and they have the means to do so," said the prosecutor.

"Cold one coming this winter." Pasquin made his slow, small talk. "Mama's Place ain't built for chilly winds."

I could feel the frigid air seeping in from the large plate glass window, from where the weather stripping had long since vacated. Mama, herself, still pushed back damp hair and mopped a sweaty upper lip. She dipped out hot blackberry cobbler into king-sized bowls, then plopped down a large pitcher of cream in front of us.

"Sit down, Mama, and have some with us." The woman looked around at the one other table with customers, then giggled and threw her pounds into a chair next to Pasquin. Her blond curls flopped onto her forehead. She looked like a female Bacchus.

"Old man, if I wasn't already hitched, I'd marry you. Cook you fish and shrimp out in that swamp house. We'd enjoy ourselves to no end of eating!" She pulled a clean saucer from the table behind her and dipped out a generous portion of the cobbler. "Been eating this stuff all morning. Don't know how I can hold anymore."

"We mustn't ask how or why, just eat and be thankful," said Pasquin, his eyes twinkling and squinting at the corners.

"It's getting colder by the minute out there. You guys really going back in that boat? Careful you don't fall in and freeze in that cold water." She poured cream until it covered the entire cobbler.

"Tell you what, my dear. Finish that cobbler and I'll take you for a ride in my boat, let you see the river from a different point of view." Pasquin smiled sweetly.

"Darling, if I get in that boat, you'll have it permanently anchored on the bottom!"

Pasquin guided his valued possession slowly away from the dock, then picked up speed as we headed back to our shores. He never revved it up to top speed. Like him, it was slow, easy, and entirely reliable. I huddled down, pulling the sweater around my nose to fend off the frigid wind. A few waterbirds flew into the cypress trees then back down to the surface to pick up a snail or a fish. There was something dead about the river. I mentioned this to Pasquin as we drifted home.

"Don't kid yourself, my dear. Life is all underground and underwater, or huddled somewhere warm right now. It's there. Just keep your eyes peeled."

We passed a cove where the river went into shallows and a path formed on the forest floor. This was a drinking spot for deer, and two were there now, both small females. Their golden brown hide invited touch, like living velvet. One spread her front legs, the white tips above the hooves almost in the water, and lowered her head to drink. The colors, dark-green and golden-brown, the water steel-black, the quiet, too quiet. The serenity broke as sudden as a gunshot. The gator leaped out of the water and gripped the deer's neck in a primitive vice. I hadn't yet sat up straight when he pulled the animal into the water and began his rollover. They tumbled, the water making death splashes that echoed through the forest. In a sudden movement, the gator headed under the surface with the dead doe. The river stayed quiet as though it kept murder a secret. The other deer fled into the protection of the trees.

Pasquin nodded, confirming his statement about life. I lifted my sweater over my nose once again, then to my eyes as I tried to blot away the tears.

"I've got something for you."

Pasquin and I sat in front of my new fireplace, logs aflame and warming away the bitter scene on the river. He handed me a box that had seen better days. "Couldn't give them to you in the regular case. Cops kept that as evidence."

I opened the lid. Inside, silver dollars piled on silver dollars. "But these are your family's inheritance."

"And just what family do you think I'm going to leave them to?"

"But you may need them one day." I picked up a few on the top, checking the dates of mint.

"Got plenty already. These are Carmina's twenty-five. You deserve them. They almost got you killed. Maybe now they can help you live."

I moved closer to the old man, his leathery face crinkled in a smile, his straw hat resting on his knee. Picking up the hat, I wondered for a moment why he carried it in the winter. It didn't matter. Putting both arms around his neck, I gave him a big hug.

"Now, now, let the old man alone."

We sipped coffee liqueur and milk by the fire and reminisced about his early life with his cousins. When he had run out of stories, he leaned back and sighed.

"You miss them, don't you?" I said.

He was quiet for a moment. "No, no I don't. We'd run out of common things years ago. They were just old ladies to me in the end."

"Poor things. They needn't have died that way."

Pasquin nodded sadly, then put his hat on his head and let me help him with his coat.

"It's dark out. Will you be okay out there on the river?"

"Always have been, child." He headed outside, pulling his collar up against the cold. Just before he left, he took my hand and said, "Say a prayer for all the little old ladies in this world. Pray they live out their years and die naturally in their beds."

I nodded, then watched him move slowly into the shadows and finally to darkness. I stood on the porch until I heard the motor start and saw the light move away from the landing. We were the spring people, would be for a long time. The folks in town call us this, and they are right. I turned off the porch light, stepped inside, and pulled the swamp around me.

For their technical assistance, gratitudes to Ken McDonald and Larry Clark of the Leon County Sheriff's Department, to Ralph Dyment of Dyment Investigations, and, for their belief in the work, to Melanie Kershaw and Cynthia Webb.

Other Memento Mori Mysteries

Matty Madrid Mysteries

MAXIMUM INSECURITY

DEADLY SIN (available Fall 2000)

by P. J. Grady

AN UNCERTAIN CURRENCY

Clyde Lynwood Sawyer, Jr.
Frances Witlin